What Readers Are Saying about Forb

"Nothing I have seen provides better spiritual equipment for today's youth to fight and win the spiritual battle raging around them than Bill Myers's Forbidden Doors series. Every Christian family should have the whole set."

C. Peter Wagner
President, Global Harvest Ministries

"During the past eighteen years as my husband and I have been involved in youth ministry, we have seen a *definite* need for these books. Bill fills the need with comedy, romance, action, and riveting suspense with clear teaching. It's a nonstop page-turner!"

Robin Jones Gunn
Author, Christy Miller series

"There is a tremendous increase of interest by teens in the occult. Everyone is exploiting and capitalizing on this hunger, but no one is providing answers. Until now. I highly recommend the Forbidden Doors series and encourage any family with teens to purchase it."

James Riordan
Music critic and author of the authorized biography of Oliver Stone

"Fast-moving, exciting, and loaded with straightforward answers to tough questions, Forbidden Doors is Bill Myers at his best."

Jon Hender
Author

The Forbidden Doors Series

#1 *The Society*
#2 *The Deceived*
#3 *The Spell*
#4 *The Haunting*
#5 *The Guardian*
#6 *The Encounter*
#7 *The Curse*
#8 *The Undead*
#9 *The Scream*
#10 *The Ancients*

FORBIDDEN DOORS

the spell

BILL MYERS

Tyndale House Publishers, Inc. Wheaton, Illinois

Visit the exciting Web site for kids at www.cool2read.com and the Forbidden Doors Web site at www.forbiddendoors.com

ISBN 0-8423-3989-2, mass paper

Printed in the United States of America

07 06 05 04
7 6 5 4

For Kenn
Gulliksen—
a pastor of love,
a teacher
of balance.

The Spirit who lives in you is greater than the spirit who lives in the world.

1 John 4:4

1

The train's light blinded Rebecca as it thundered toward her. She lay on her back and felt the locomotive's power vibrating through the tracks. It was nearly there. She could smell the diesel fuel, see the massive wheels rolling at her. She opened her mouth to scream, but no sound came out. There was only the shriek of the train's whistle.

The wheels were nearly on top of her. She tried to move, but the IV tubes kept her pinned to the hospital bed.

IV tubes? Hospital bed?

With a jolt, Becka woke up. She fought to catch her breath. Her eyes darted around the room. There was no train, no glaring light. Only the muted glow from the lights in the hospital parking lot as they shone through her curtains.

With a groan, she fell back against her pillows. It was another dream. Another one of *those* dreams. The type she'd been having every night for the last week. Ever since her little accident with the train.

She adjusted her hospital gown. It was damp with sweat and stuck to her back.

The shrinks (you don't stand in front of a racing train in the middle of the night, almost getting yourself killed, without a few psychiatrists dropping by) said the dreams weren't unusual. After running about a thousand tests on Becka, they assured her she was going to be all right. "Other than major trauma from the accident, and scoring slightly below average in the area of self-esteem, you seem to be a perfectly normal teenager."

Becka didn't feel "perfectly normal." Last week's run-in with the train—and with Maxwell Hunter, the hotshot New Ager—had left her a little shaky. Actually, a *lot* shaky. Maxwell was an acclaimed speaker on reincarnation. To prove his theories of past lives, he had hypnotized Becka in front of an audience and taken her back to her "past lives."

At first Becka bought it. It all seemed so believable . . . right up to the end. Right up until she realized the past lives were nothing but demons playing a game with her mind.

But that was all behind her now. Ancient history. The doctors had assured her she was "all right" and "perfectly normal." And if the doctors said that was so, who was she to disagree?

She turned her head on the pillow and looked through the stainless-steel rails of her hospital bed. The digital clock on the nightstand glowed a crimson 3:01. Four hours and fifty-nine minutes left before she could go home. Four hours and fifty-nine minutes before she was finally out of there.

Her eyes drifted from the clock to the get-well cards on the dresser, then stopped at the giant bouquet of carnations. Even in the dim light, she could make out the flowers' vivid reds and whites. Fear from the dream melted, dissolving into a pool of warmth, a glow of happiness that stirred deep inside her chest. It was too dark to read the card attached to the carnations, but she didn't have to. She knew it by heart:

Hurry and get well. I really miss you.
Your buddy, Ryan

She could have lived without the "your buddy" part. Other phrases would have been much better. Actually, one specific word—the *L* word—would have done the trick. But the sentence "I really miss you" rang in Becka's heart as resoundingly as when she'd first read it:

"I *REALLY* miss you."

"I really *MISS* you."

"I really miss *YOU.*"

The glow in her chest spread through her body. She felt cozy all over as she snuggled deeper under the covers. Ryan said he might be there when Mom and Scotty, her little brother, picked her up in the morning. She hoped so.

She glanced at the clock and closed her eyes, smiling. 3:02. Four hours and fifty-eight minutes . . .

The six robed figures stood in a secluded clearing of the park. All around them were dense trees and overgrown bushes, making it impossible to see them from the road. This was good. This was exactly what they wanted.

As usual for this time of year, the fog had rolled in from the beach and blotted out all light from the moon. This was good, too. Now there was only the glow of six candles—five black, one white—on the picnic table, their orange light flickering and dancing over the young faces around them.

There were two boys and four girls. Teenagers. Dressed in homemade robes, complete with hoods. All of the group had been drinking, and the boys' red, watery eyes gave clear signs that they'd been smoking dope. Lots of it.

The rat had already been killed, its neck broken. Now the group's leader, Brooke, a chunky girl whose black hair was an obvious dye job, carefully drained the animal's blood, filling the bottom half of a torn diet Coke can with the dark liquid.

The boys snickered. It may have been from the booze or the dope or just from the chill of what they were doing. Who knew? But it was obvious they weren't taking the ceremony seriously.

Laura Henderson, a brooding blonde whose face was ravaged by acne, gave them a scowl. This was important business. After all,

Brooke had called this meeting and was making this sacrifice for a very serious reason. She had been humiliated—not once, but twice! By a couple of zeros who'd moved into the neighborhood barely a month ago. First there was the younger kid, Scott Williams. He'd actually dared to challenge their leader's powers with the Ouija board. And he'd done it right in front of the entire Society!

Then there was the sister, Rebecca Williams . . . as plain as they come. And yet, for some reason, she had been handpicked by the famous guru, Maxwell Hunter, for her supposed gifts. How did such a nobody rate that kind of honor? As if that wasn't bad enough, there was that stunt Williams had pulled with the train—proof to all that Rebecca Williams was trying to compete with Brooke's power and position.

Laura turned and watched with admiration as Brooke finished draining the rat's blood into the can. Brooke meant everything to her. She lived for the girl's praise, wilted at her criticism. She glanced around at the group circling the candles. As her eyes returned to Brooke, her expression hardened.

OK, Williams, you want power? So be it. We'll show *you power.*

She closed her eyes and began to recite: "Hate your enemies with your whole heart . . ."

The other two girls joined in. The chant grew louder, more concentrated: ". . . and if a man smite you on the cheek, *smash* him on the other!"

The boys smirked and snickered. Laura opened her eyes and cut them an icy glare. After another snicker and a shrug of indifference they also joined in.

"Hate your enemies with your whole heart, and if a man smite you on the cheek, *smash* him on the other!"

Brooke set the rat carcass on the picnic table and reached into her robe, pulling out a feathered quill and a piece of homemade parchment.

The chant continued.

"Hate your enemies with your whole heart . . ."

Brooke dipped the quill into the can of blood.

". . . and if a man smite you on the cheek, *smash* him on the other!"

And then she wrote:

Rebecca

"Hate your enemies with your whole heart . . ."

". . . and if a man smite you on the cheek, *smash* him on the other!"

Their voices grew louder. The booze, the drugs, the force of six people chanting together—it all gave them a kind of energy, a sense of belonging. Laura drew a deep breath and felt a surge of exhilaration. The chant grew stronger, more determined, filling the air, filling her being. This was the unity she needed, the power she craved.

"Hate your enemies with your whole heart . . ."

Brooke set the pen down and raised the parchment above the flame of the white candle. The chanting grew more and more feverish. All eyes watched now in eager anticipation.

". . . and if a man smite you on the cheek, smash *him on the other!"*

Suddenly the parchment ignited into a bright orange flame. The paper curled and crackled as it was consumed, quickly and efficiently, until everything—including Rebecca's name—was nothing but ash.

"Why so glum, sweetheart?" Mom asked as she turned their clunker Toyota onto their street and headed toward the house.

Rebecca stared out the window at the passing homes. Theirs wasn't the poorest neighborhood in town, but it wasn't the richest either. Usually she didn't notice the sagging screens, the peeling paint, the semikept yards. But today she did. Today they bugged her. Today everything bugged her.

For good reason. What had started out as such a great morning had already turned into a major disaster.

First, Mom was late getting to the hospital. Almost an hour late. Second, nobody came with her. Not Ryan, not even Scotty. Obviously their lives were far too busy to squeeze her into their schedule. But that was small potatoes compared to the third reason, the one crammed into the Toyota's trunk.

"You still embarrassed about the wheelchair?" Mom asked.

Becka said nothing.

"The doctors say it'll only be for a few weeks."

More silence.

"If you'd just broken your leg, you could use crutches, but—"

Becka impatiently interrupted, "But since I cracked my collarbone, I can't put the extra weight on my shoulders. I know, Mother. I was there, remember?" Becka bit her lip. She hated being a jerk. She knew

Mom was only trying to cheer her up. But still . . .

And then she saw it: the white vintage Mustang parked in front of their house. "Ryan's here!" she blurted.

"Well, what do you know." Mom threw Becka a knowing smile.

Becka grinned back, realizing her mother was part of a conspiracy. For not only was Ryan's car there, but so was her best friend Julie's Jeep and Philip's burgundy convertible. Instinctively, her hand shot up to her thin brown hair, fluffing it out, trying in vain to make it look halfway presentable.

The Toyota turned and rattled up the driveway. Mom turned it off, and after a couple shuddering coughs, the engine finally died.

Little brother Scott was the first to spot them. Not that he was so little anymore. In the last couple of months, he had almost caught up to Becka's height. And by his cracking voice and thickening shoulders, it was clear that manhood was lurking just around the corner.

"She's here," Scott called as he threw open the porch door and clambered down the steps. The others piled out after him. First there was Scott's dorky friend, Darryl. Then Becka's best friend, the athletic and always-too-beautiful-and-perfectly-dressed Julie, followed closely by Ryan, who sported a devilish grin. Finally, there were Philip and his airhead girlfriend, Krissi (better known as Ken and Barbie).

Rebecca could feel her ears start to burn and color run to her cheeks. This was the first time most of them had seen where she lived. Not that she was trying to keep it a secret, but let's face it, this was definitely not one of those hotsy-totsy country-club homes they were used to.

Still, as they headed toward the car, throwing jibes and barbs, she saw no signs of snobbery.

"Hey there, Crash, how you feeling?" Ryan brushed the thick black hair out of his gorgeous blue eyes. And if that wasn't enough, he suddenly flashed her his triple-A heartbreaker smile.

"Great," Becka answered with a grin as she pushed open the car door. She wasn't lying, either. Suddenly, she *was* feeling better—a whole lot better.

"I'll get the wheelchair," Mom called.

Suddenly, she was feeling worse—a whole lot worse.

"Wheelchair?" Julie echoed.

"Just for a few weeks," Mom explained as she crossed back to the trunk and opened it.

"Don't tell me we've got to push her around like some old duffer," Scott groaned.

Good ol' Scotty. *Thanks for the support, little brother.*

"Just a few weeks," Mom repeated as she unfolded the chair.

"Here, I can get that," Ryan said, quickly moving in to take it from her.

"That's cool." Philip grinned at Becka. "That means we can, like, escort you all around, then."

Krissi laughed, "The queen on her portable throne."

Ryan hammed it up as he rolled the chair toward her open car door. "And I, her loyal servant, shall take her wherever she bids." Before Becka could protest, he swooped down and scooped her from the car seat and into his arms. Then, ever so gently, he set her into the chair. "Welcome home." He grinned. Becka felt her heart do a little flip-flop.

When she had first met Ryan, she agreed with Mom that they could hang out as friends. But as far as any "official" dating or boyfriend/girlfriend thing—no way. It made no difference how many back flips her heart did when she saw him or that he just happened to be the cutest and nicest guy in school (no prejudice there). The point is she was a Christian and he was not. And until that changed, she knew it was best to guard her heart and simply remain good friends.

But still . . .

Ryan pulled the chair away from the car and started pushing Becka toward the open garage. Everyone followed, talking and making jokes, while Krissi, once again proving her incredible airheadedness, asked, "Does this mean you won't be running in any more track meets?"

More laughter and wisecracks as they passed through the dozens of stacked boxes in the garage and headed toward the kitchen door.

"So this is the famous haunted garage?" Philip asked as he slowed to a stop and glanced around.

"It doesn't look so scary," Krissi chirped.

"Not in the daylight," Scott said. "But try hanging out here at night."

"All alone," Darryl added, pushing up his glasses and giving a little sniff, "with all those sounds and that light and stuff."

And then, as if on cue, there was a gentle whine. Becka stiffened. Even now, with all these people around, she was still a little skittish. "Did you hear that?" she asked.

"Hear what?" Ryan asked.

The sound repeated itself: a high-pitched whine, accompanied by scratching.

"Don't you hear that?" she asked.

Ryan looked puzzled, then shook his head. "You guys hear anything?"

Everyone quieted down and listened.

"I don't hear a thing," Philip said.

"Me neither," Krissi said.

Becka looked up to their faces and fought off a shiver.

The sound recurred.

"There." Becka pointed toward the closed kitchen door. "It's coming from behind there."

"Here?" Ryan asked as they rolled to a stop in front of the door.

The scratching and whining grew louder.

"Can't you guys hear that?" Rebecca demanded.

There were more baffled looks, this time accompanied by some raised eyebrows of concern. "We, uh, we don't hear anything, Beck," Julie ventured cautiously.

The scratching grew louder. "Guys—" Becka tried to smile, thinking it was some kind of joke—"you mean to tell me none of you hear that?"

But no one smiled back. She shifted uneasily, her fear and self-doubt starting to grow.

Ryan dropped to his knees and put his ear to the door. "You're talking about this door, right here?"

"Yes," Becka said, fighting off her impatience. "There's something behind it. Can't you hear that?"

Cautiously, Ryan reached up to the knob and turned it. It was unlocked. He looked at Becka, then, suddenly, he threw open the door.

Becka gasped as a little ball of black-and-brown fur scampered out and leaped into Ryan's arms. It immediately began covering the boy with slobbery licks and kisses. "Easy, fella," Ryan laughed. "Down boy, easy."

"You guys!" Becka cried as a wave of relief washed over her. She watched as the puppy continued washing Ryan's face. "He's so cute. What kind is he?" she asked.

"Got me," Ryan said, trying in vain to dodge the wayward tongue. "Heinz 57, a mix of everything." He stood up and placed the squirming bundle of fur on Becka's lap. It took the animal half a second to find her face and resume the licking.

The group laughed and Becka giggled, trying to fight off the kissing attack. "Where'd he come from? Whose is he?"

"He's yours," Julie laughed. "Ryan got him from the pound."

The kitchen phone started ringing, but Becka barely heard. She looked up to Ryan. His eyes were sparkling with delight. He said only four words, and they were so soft no one else heard: "I'm glad you're back."

She reached out and took his hand. "Thank you," she whispered. His eyes sparkled even brighter. As far as Rebecca was concerned, the moment could last forever. Unfortunately there was Krissi. "Do you like him?" she blurted. "Hey, Becka, do you like him?"

"Like him?" Rebecca looked back down to the pup and was met with another licking attack. "I *love* him."

Everyone moved in, kneeling and petting the animal who grew even more hyper from all the attention.

"What are you going to call him?" Julie asked. She leaned in and was met with a wet tongue right across the mouth. "Oh, gross." More laughter.

"What am I going to call him?" Rebecca giggled. She paused a moment to look him over. Ryan was right, the little scamp was a mix of just about every breed of dog imaginable. "What am I going to call him? . . . How about . . . 'Muttly.'"

Everyone agreed. It was the perfect name.

Suddenly Scott was shoving the cordless phone through the crowd of faces toward her. He looked a little perplexed. "It's for you," he said.

Still laughing and still fighting off the puppy, Becka took the receiver. “Hello?”

At first there was no response.

“Hello?” she repeated.

Then came the voice. It was low and raspy. “The spell has been cast, Rebecca Williams.”

“I’m sorry?” She motioned for the others to quiet down. “What did you say?”

Now she heard the voice distinctly. “The spell has been cast. . . . Your destiny belongs to me.”

Rebecca swallowed. It took a moment for her to speak. “Who—who is this? What are you talking about?”

There was no answer, only the click of the receiver followed by the dial tone.

2

It was Thursday morning—Becka's first day back at school. Ryan had kept his word about playing chauffeur. He had shown up bright and early and was helping her into the front seat of his Mustang. She was nervous about returning to school. Real nervous. Call it a wild hunch, but she figured standing on railroad tracks and waiting to get hit by a train had probably started a few people gossiping about her. Then, of course, there was the little welcome-home phone call she had received: *Your destiny belongs to me.*

Ryan sensed her tension and tried to keep things light. "So how's Muttly?" he asked as he slid in behind the wheel.

"Great," Becka said, trying too hard to be cheery. "Well, except for the whining and whimpering and scratching all night long."

"Sorry about that," Ryan chuckled. He started up the car and pulled into the street. "Maybe you should keep him in the garage at night."

"I couldn't do that," Becka protested.

"Why not?"

"He'd get too lonely. Besides . . ." She hesitated, unsure how to continue.

"Besides, what?"

"Well, you know."

Ryan threw her a mischievous look. "You mean the Haunted Garage?"

Becka half shrugged.

"Come on, Beck, you really don't buy into all that ghost stuff."

Rebecca took a deep breath and finally spoke her mind. "It's not just the garage. . . ."

Ryan glanced back to her. She said nothing, but he knew what she was thinking.

"You're still worried about that phone call?"

Becka looked down and nodded.

Ryan answered, "It's just a bad joke someone is playing. Don't let it bug you. Besides, aren't Christians supposed to be protected from curses and all that junk?"

Rebecca turned to him in surprise. "How'd you know I was a Christian?"

He chuckled. "That stuff's kinda hard to hide."

She continued to stare.

"Hey, relax." He smiled. "I think it's cool. I mean, I wish I had something like that to believe in." Becka noticed the slightest trace of sadness in his voice. He shrugged. "Maybe we can take in church together sometime—you know, have you show me the ropes."

You could have knocked her over with a feather. Who was this guy who never ceased to amaze her? He glanced at her and smiled again. It was the killer smile—the one that caused her heart to flutter. He looked down to her hand and reached for it. The flip-flops increased.

Suddenly something caught Becka's attention. A fat tabby cat darted off the curb directly in front of them. "Look out!" she cried.

Ryan looked up, his eyes widening. He

swerved hard to the left, barely missing the animal. The car slid, and for a brief second Becka looked out her window to see she was heading directly for a parked car. She started to scream, bracing herself for the crash, but Ryan managed to straighten his car, missing the parked one by only a few inches.

He quickly pulled to a stop. "You all right?" he asked in concern.

Becka took a deep breath to steady herself.

"Beck?"

She took another breath. "Yeah . . . I'm fine."

"You sure?"

She nodded.

He looked at her a long moment before putting the car into gear and slowly pulling away.

She was still shaken. The past few days—make that the past few weeks—had definitely taken their toll. Still, she tried to make a joke. "You were saying something about curses?"

Ryan forced a laugh. "Good thing that cat wasn't black."

Becka didn't return the laugh.

Once again Ryan looked at her with concern. "Beck . . . not everything that goes bump in the night is the devil. Just because stuff goes wrong doesn't mean something's out to get you." He flashed her a reassuring smile. "That's why they call them accidents."

Becka took another breath and tried to smile back. She wanted to answer, but she didn't trust her voice. *I hope you're right* was all she could think. *I just hope you're right.*

Scott had barely entered Crescent Bay High when Darryl joined him. As usual, his little dorky friend was sniffing, pushing up his glasses, and rattling on about something . . . and, as usual, Scott, the nice guy, was trying his best to be interested. Trying, but not succeeding. Then he heard his name:

"Scott . . . Scott, wait up."

He turned to see a gorgeous redhead maneuvering her way through the crowded hallway toward him. They'd met before. At the Ascension Bookshop. Even then he remembered thinking she looked incredible—shoulder-length copper hair, beautiful green eyes, mischievous smile. Of course, at the time, he had been a little preoccupied with fighting Ouija boards and casting out demons to pay too much attention.

"Hi." She smiled as she bounced up next to him and flipped her hair to the side. "I'm Kara. We met at the Society a couple of weeks back." Before Scott could answer she leaned past him and offered a perky "Hi" to Darryl.

"Hi," Darryl's voice squeaked. Darryl's voice always squeaked—especially when he talked to gorgeous girls. At the moment he sounded halfway between a rusty hinge and a cat stuck in the dryer.

She turned her attention back to Scott. "How've you been?" she asked, sounding as if they'd been friends for years.

"Pretty good," he answered.

"Great."

They walked on in silence. Scott wasn't sure what was going on, but he figured if he waited long enough, he'd find out.

"Sorry about your sister," Kara offered. "But I heard she's out of the hospital now."

"Yeah," Scott said, still waiting. Then another thought came to mind. And with the thought, a trace of anger. "Listen, you guys in the Society, you're not the ones who called her when she got home, are you?"

"Called her?" Kara asked.

Scott looked at her carefully. "Yeah, something about casting a spell and taking away her destiny."

Kara shook her head. She was still light and breezy, but there was also a trace of sadness to her voice. "No, that wasn't us . . . at least it wasn't me."

"But you know something about it?"

"I know that Brooke is pretty mad about all the attention your sister's been getting."

"Brooke?"

"Yeah, you know, the leader of the Society. And I know that she and a few of the kids are getting real heavy into this satanism."

"Satanism?" Scott asked.

"Yeah."

"But not you, huh?"

Kara laughed, "No way."

Scott glanced at her. She sure seemed to be telling the truth. "Well," he continued, "if you should happen to see Brooke, tell her to lay off, will you? Becka's pretty shook already, and she doesn't need somebody playing with her mind."

"I will, Scott." Kara held his gaze. "You have my word on it. I'll definitely tell her."

There was something about the sincerity in Kara's voice and the twinkle in her jade green eyes that caught Scott off guard, that made him realize he was definitely mad at the wrong person. It also made him realize it was time to change gears and dig up some of that world-famous Scott Williams charm. "Hey, how 'bout the homework Mr. Patton is laying on us?" he asked.

"Yeah," Kara said, suddenly sounding as chipper as ever. "That's what I want to talk to you about." She nodded to a couple of passing boys and continued, "I was wondering—I mean, you're so good at algebra and everything—could you . . . I mean, could we, like, get together sometime, and maybe you could . . . tutor me a little?"

For a split second Scott was surprised. Then came the grin. He'd heard rumors about California girls and how forward they could be, but he'd never seen one in action. *Tutor her? Who's she kidding?* He knew a come-on when he heard one. But that's OK; if that's how the game was played, he could play it as well as the next guy.

"Sure," he said slowly, pretending to think over her request. "I'm sure we could, you know, work something out."

"Great!" She beamed, then suddenly spun on her heels and headed off in the opposite direction. "I'll give you a call."

"Yeah, right—," Scott said, trying to cover his surprise. "You give me a call." He continued to stare after her, marveling, until Darryl brought him back to reality with one of his irritating sniffs.

"You're good," Darryl said, shaking his head in admiration. "Real good."

"Yeah," Scott chuckled, although he still

wasn't sure what he had done or how he had done it, "I guess I am pretty smooth."

Becka's face was on fire as Ryan wheeled her through the doors of Crescent Bay High. She'd known returning to school would be tough. She just hadn't known it would be *this* tough.

As they started down the hall it reminded her of the old Ten Commandments movie where Moses parts the Red Sea. Ryan pushed her through the crowd and everyone stepped back, giving her space. One or two murmured a greeting, but most just stopped talking and stared. Those in the front looked down at her and gawked, while those in the back shifted for a better view.

Rebecca bit her lip and stared hard at her lap. Maybe getting smashed on the train tracks wouldn't have been such a bad idea after all.

"Look up," Ryan whispered, so softly that she almost didn't hear. She wanted to glance at him, to confirm what he'd said, but she was too embarrassed.

"I said look up." His voice was firmer now, yet just as gentle. "I'm right here with you, Becka. You have nothing to be ashamed of. Look up."

Rebecca stared even harder at her lap, hoping no one would hear him.

"Becka . . ."

His voice was louder now. She wanted him to shut up. Didn't he know he was asking the impossible? Didn't he know that she was incapable of looking up?

"Don't let them do this to you," he said. "You're just as good as they are. Look into their faces."

Why was he pushing? Why didn't he just let her be? Why didn't he let her melt into the wheelchair? Then she heard another voice: Julie's.

"Hey, Rebecca! Welcome back to the living!" Becka stole a glance and saw her best friend making her way through the crowd toward her. Julie was all smiles, just as bright and cheery as if nothing had ever happened. "I love that sweater," she said as if seeing her friend in a wheelchair was an everyday occurrence. Before Becka could respond, Julie had joined her and Ryan, and was walking along with them. Suddenly she spotted a kid from student council—one of the most popular guys in school. She flashed him her cover girl smile. "Hey Brian, have you met my good friend Becka Williams?"

Brian stared.

"Well, have you?" she persisted.

"Uh, no . . . not yet."

"Then come over and say hi. She's pretty cool."

He hesitated.

If Becka thought she'd been dying of embarrassment before, she knew it was time to start planning the funeral now. *What are you trying to prove?* she thought. *Aren't we friends? Why are you doing this to me?*

But Julie pressed on. "Don't be shy," she said to Brian, her voice teasing. She motioned to him. "Come on."

Brian threw a look at his buddy, shrugged, then pushed through the crowd to join them, falling in step beside Julie, Ryan, and the wheelchair.

But before introductions were made, Julie was calling out to somebody else. "Karen, I want you to meet Rebecca Williams. She's the one who gave up her position at the track prelims so I could win. Remember?"

"Yeah, I heard."

"Come over here and meet her."

The girl hesitated, but Julie's persistence and cheerfulness were overpowering. "Come on, it'll only take a minute."

If there was one thing Karen could tell, it was when something important was happening. And if there was one thing Karen hated, it was being left out of anything important. So she joined them.

Now there were five.

A lump swelled in the back of Becka's throat. She looked up at Julie, appreciation washing over her. Her friend was cashing in on her popularity to build up Becka's acceptability.

"Hey, Philip, Krissi," Ryan called out. "Look who I've got!"

"I see," Krissi chirped as she pulled Philip through the crowd toward them. "You look terrific, Becka," she said loud enough for everyone to hear. She turned to Philip and continued, "Doesn't she look terrific?"

Philip nodded as they joined the procession. "She's right, Beck, you look great."

Becka's face was still on fire, but there was no missing the moisture of gratitude filling her eyes. Just like the day she'd come home from the hospital, this had been a conspiracy from the beginning. Something they had planned all along. Her friends were standing up for her, making it clear she was not a freak or some nutsoid crazy.

And if they could go out on a limb for her, then the least she could do was hold her head up for them. She raised her eyes. She wouldn't lower her gaze again. Not now. Not after all they were doing for her. Instead, she met the curious gazes around her head-on. She stared back at those who were staring, at those who were murmuring—and she held their gazes until they were the ones who suddenly grew uncomfortable and looked down.

By the time they arrived at her locker, Becka was feeling a thousand percent better.

"I told you there was nothing to be embarrassed about," Ryan said, playfully nudging Becka's head as she dialed her combination.

She laughed, "You guys really pulled out the big guns."

Julie grinned. "For you, kiddo, anything."

Becka looked at her, then to Ryan, and finally to the others. She tried to hide her emotion with a smile. But when she spoke, her voice was hoarse. "Thanks, guys."

"No sweat." Philip shrugged.

Becka turned back to her locker and opened the door. It was so great to have friends like—

Her smile froze. She wanted to scream, but no sound came. She wanted to gasp, but she could not breathe. Instead, she started to shake. All over.

There, on the center coat hook, hanging from a string by its broken neck, was a dead rat. A note was pinned to the carcass. Scrawled writing, which looked like it was in blood, read:

YOUR DESTINY IS MINE.

3

Cornelius strutted back and forth on his perch in agitation.

"MAKE MY DAY, PUNK! *SQUAWK!* MAKE MY DAY, MAKE MY DAY!"

The reason for his anger was simple: Muttly. Obviously the little fur ball hadn't read the handbook on puppyhood. Especially the part that says dogs and parrots are not best friends. It seemed no matter what Cornelius did, Muttly would find him, sneak up on him, and start yapping in delight—which always sent the bird flapping and squawking back to his perch in horror.

It was all fun and games for Muttly, who now sat on his haunches, panting and grinning for joy. But it was sheer terror for Cornelius, who paced back and forth, screeching at the top of his lungs.

"MAKE MY DAY, PUNK! MAKE MY DAY, MAKE MY DAY! *SQUAWK!*"

Rebecca laughed as she patted her lap for the puppy to join her in the wheelchair. "Come here, boy, come on." Muttly scampered up her leg and into her lap. Immediately he set his wet tongue into action. "OK, fellow, settle down," she said, trying to avoid the kisses.

After turning several tight circles and going through plenty more squirmings and lickings, he finally found his place—perched as far up Becka's chest as he could go, snuggling in as far under her chin as he could get. Becka could feel his tiny puffs of warm breath, and when she remained still, she could feel his little heart tripping away.

She treasured this little guy. Not just

because he was from Ryan, but because he never seemed to run out of love. No matter what she did, or failed to do, Muttly was always there with his wagging tail and busy tongue.

Right then, they were with Scott in his room, sitting near his computer. "It's almost nine," she said. "Shouldn't Z be logging on?"

Scott nodded. He was munching on a piece of day-old pizza as he slid into the chair behind his desk and snapped on the computer. "Don't get too disappointed if he's not there," he said. "I mean it's not like he calls every night." Scott entered the chat room. He clicked the mouse a couple of times.

"You really think he'll know about the rat and the threats and stuff?" Becka asked, watching.

"He hasn't let us down yet."

Scott had a point. Whether it was Ouija boards, reincarnation, or just your basic, run-of-the-mill demonic possession—if it was anything dealing with things supernatural—somehow Z knew about it. But he knew more than that. He knew about Becka and Scott. Their personal lives. They'd never met him (not that they hadn't tried), and he would only talk to them through the computer network, but somehow, someway, he always knew what they were up to. Sometimes it was comforting.

Other times it was eerie. Real eerie.

Scott began typing:

Z, are you there?

They both waited, staring at the screen. There was no answer. Muttly gave a little whine and snuggled closer under Becka's chin. She scratched behind his ears.

Z, it's New Kid—are you there?

More waiting. Finally the words appeared:

Hello, New Kid. How's Rebecca?

Becka swallowed. It was strange to watch people communicate like this, and it was definitely unnerving to see her name typed up on the screen by someone she didn't even know.

Scott typed back:

Today was her first day of school.

I know. I'm glad her friends are helping her get adjusted.

Scott threw a look over to Becka and

shook his head in amazement. Was there anything this guy didn't know? Becka took a slow, deep breath, then spoke. "Ask him about the note and stuff. Ask him what your redheaded friend said about them being satanists."

Scott turned back to the keyboard and typed:

Z, what do you know about satanism?

The response formed:

Are you being bothered by the Society again?
Not the whole group. Just some kids who claim to be satanists. What do you know about them?

There was no answer. Scott typed:

Z . . . are you there? Z?

Finally, the response came:

I believe satanists are given more credit than they deserve.
How's that?
For the most part, satanists are outcasts who find it difficult to fit in to society. So they indulge in drugs, sex, music, anything leading to self-gratification.

Scott quickly fired back:

What about human sacrifices and curses and spells and that sort of stuff?

Opinion is divided. Many so-called satanists are usually looking for a shortcut to control and power. They feel their ceremonies provide them with those things. Others are just in it for the thrill. But as for actual spiritual authority, I have strong doubts they can do anything supernatural.

"I don't know about that," Becka said. "Tell him I disagree." Scott nodded and typed:

Becka has her doubts.

The words formed:

Hello, Rebecca.

She fought back a wave of uneasiness. This was the first time Z had directly addressed her. The words continued:

After your ordeal I can appreciate your fears. But understand that everything that goes wrong is not necessarily satanic or supernatural. I believe the only power satanists have is the power you give them through your fear.

Before Rebecca could respond Scott typed:

What about the human sacrifices we always hear about?

They are very, very rare.

But possible?

There was a pause, then the words formed:

Why haven't you two started attending church?

Scott threw a look to Becka and typed:

Are you changing the subject?

Yes.

"Well, at least he's honest," Scott sighed. He typed the words:

I guess we haven't had the time with moving in and all that's been happening. Besides, we've got each other and Mom . . . and, of course, the great Z, our private answer man.

The response quickly returned:

I am no substitute for surrounding yourself with other believers. You need them for growth. You should also have a place you can invite your friends to visit.

Becka fought off a little shiver. Wasn't it just this morning that Ryan had mentioned going to church with her? "Ask him—" She took a breath. "Ask him how he knew."

Scott turned back to her. "What?"

"Ask him how he knew about Ryan."

"What are you talking—"

She cut him off. "Just ask!"

Scott turned back to the computer and typed:

Becka wants to know how you knew about Ryan.

There was another pause. And finally:

Good night, you two.

Quickly Scott typed:

Z . . . Z . . . don't go yet! Z?

There was no response. "He's gone." Scott leaned back in his chair and sighed, "I hate it when he does that."

Becka stared at the screen, feeling colder than ever. "Me, too," she muttered, pulling Muttly closer. "Me, too."

It was three o'clock in the morning when the phone rang. Scott, who was known for his weird dreams, was in the middle of a doozy: He was giving an oral book report on *A Tale of Two Cities* to a classroom full of all the world leaders. Nothing too unusual there, except that he was dressed only in his Fruit Of The Looms.

The phone continued ringing until he awoke. Grateful for the interruption (he hadn't even read the book), he threw off the covers and stumbled across his room to the phone.

"Hello?" he mumbled.

"Scott, is that you?"

"I think so. Who's this?"

"Kara."

"Kara?"

"From algebra."

There was a click on the line as Mom's sleepy voice answered from the extension. "Hello?"

"It's OK, Mom, I got it."

"Oh," Mom answered drowsily.

"Hi, Mrs. Williams," Kara said cheerily. "I'm Kara."

"Oh," Mom repeated, obviously still asleep, "that's nice."

There was a pause. Finally Scott spoke. "Good night, Mom."

"Oh," Mom said a third time, "good night." There was a loud clunking as Mom struggled to find the phone cradle and a click as she finally hung up.

"Scott," Kara began, "I talked to Brooke early this evening."

"Can't this wait till tomorrow?" Scott asked, rubbing his eyes, trying to clear the last of the world leaders out of his mind.

"I asked her if she was the one putting the curse on your sister."

Suddenly Scott was wide awake. "And?"

"And she said no."

"So that's good."

"Not necessarily. It was the way she said it: 'Us not is it.' "

"What?"

"She was speaking backwards. Sometimes they do that. It could mean just the opposite of what she said."

"So . . . she was lying?" Scott frowned, trying to bring the pieces together.

"I wasn't sure, so I tried to call her just now to see if she was home. She wasn't."

"What's that got to do with—"

"Usually when they make their sacrifices and cast their spells it's around three in the morning."

Scott's eyes darted to his clock radio: 3:16. Then, out of the corner of his eye, he saw someone in the doorway. He spun around to see Becka sitting in her wheelchair. Even in the dim light he could see how concerned she was. And how frightened. He covered the mouthpiece and asked, "Hey, Beck, what's up?"

She said only three words. They were exactly the ones he didn't want to hear: "You tell me."

The cemetery was covered in a thick, cold fog. Tiny droplets of water collected on the kids' clothes and heads, condensing into larger drops that streamed down their coats and faces. There was only one light, a single neon vapor that hung from a pole above the adjacent Community Church parking lot. The fog absorbed most of it before it reached the open grave. Not only did the fog absorb the light, but it muffled the clanks and thuds of the pickax and shovel, too.

"How much farther?" Brooke demanded as she shone her flashlight into a hole at the boys.

The two guys leaned against their digging tools, waist deep in the pit, gasping for breath. At first the idea of sneaking into a graveyard and digging up a corpse sounded pretty exciting. But now, between the booze, the freezing fog, and the heavy clay dirt that resisted every hit of the pickax and shovel, both the excitement and the guys' strength were gone.

"Should be any time," the meatier of the two boys growled. The other guy, a kid with a shaved head and more earrings than a jewelry store, looked at him doubtfully. But he didn't say anything. He knew what happened when Meaty Guy drank, and there was no way he was going to become the brunt of all that anger.

He watched as Meaty Guy wiped the cold moisture from his face, raised the pickax over his head, and gave another swing.

Thud.

Without a word, Shaved Head resumed his digging.

Not far away, Laura, the acne-ravaged blonde, was knocking over small upright tombstones. Brooke had nodded in grim approval when the first one toppled, so Laura continued. Some of the markers were easy. Others took five, six, even seven kicks before they broke and fell. It was something Laura would never do on her own. But the whiskey and the approval in Brooke's eyes had opened new doors for her. Now, as each tombstone collapsed, she felt a little surge of power.

Two other girls stood across the hole from Brooke. The younger and more frail looking of the two shivered when she spoke. "Brooke?" Her voice was thin and slurred. "Can I wait in the car? I don't feel so good."

Brooke shot her a look that made the girl cringe.

"Here," her friend said, producing a half-empty bottle of Jack Daniel's from her parka. "Have some more. It'll keep you warm."

Frail Girl took the bottle and eyed it warily. She wasn't so much cold as she was sick, and she was pretty sure the whiskey wasn't going to help in that department. But she couldn't refuse. Not with the others, especially Brooke, watching her. She tilted her head back and drank. It was all she could do to keep from gagging.

"Aughh!" Meaty Guy grunted.

"What?" Brooke flashed the light back into the hole but saw nothing except the damp clay and some darker earth.

"It's what's left of a coffin." He raised his pick above his head and slammed it down hard. The dark dirt gave way more easily. Everyone moved in for a closer look. "Give me that shovel," Meaty Guy ordered.

His partner handed him the shovel. Meaty Guy carefully scooped three, four, five shovelfuls out of the way. Suddenly, the flashlight caught a reflection of whiteness.

"Is it—?" Shaved Head asked.

"Yeah," Meaty Guy muttered. "A bone."

"Brooke." It was Frail Girl again. This time her speech was worse. "I don't feel so good . . . really. . . ."

No one paid attention. Meaty Guy continued to dig. By now, Laura had also joined the group as they crowded closer to the hole and peered in.

At last Meaty Guy kneeled down. He carefully brushed aside some clay, then took something into his hand. Everyone stared as he slowly rose to his feet. Much of it was still covered in dirt, but there was no missing the gleaming white bone and the two hollow eye sockets.

"Give it to me," Brooke commanded. Meaty Guy reached up and handed her the skull.

The group looked on, enjoying the thrill, the cold tingling that spread through their bodies. No one spoke. The skull repulsed and attracted, frightened and excited. Everyone stared in cautious awe. Everyone but Frail Girl. She dropped to all fours and began to vomit. Deep, gut-wrenching gags, so loud that they set a neighbor's dog to barking.

Laura looked down at her with disgust. She hated weakness. She knew Brooke did, too.

Brooke pulled the skull into her parka and ordered, "Come on, we've got lots to do." She turned, and everyone but Frail Girl headed toward the beat-up Nissan in the church parking lot.

When Frail Girl finally looked up, she realized in terror that she was being left alone at the open grave. "Wait for me!" she cried. "Wait!" She wiped her mouth, struggled to her feet, and staggered after them.

When they arrived at the Nissan, Laura reached into the backseat and pulled out a paper bag. Brooke was gonna love this.

"What's that?" Meaty Guy asked.

"I'll be right back," Laura said. She produced a couple of cans of black spray paint from the bag. They made clicking sounds as she shook them back and forth and started toward the church. "I just want to pay my respects to somebody." She threw a quick look to Brooke, who broke into a grin. Laura's heart swelled.

"Wait a minute," Brooke commanded. "Let's all go."

It was Friday. School had just let out. Ryan pushed Rebecca through the front doors and prepared to ease both her and the wheelchair down the dozen or so steps to the sidewalk. Suddenly she looked up from rummaging in her backpack and groaned, “Oh no.”

“What’s wrong?”

"I forgot my chemistry book."

"No sweat." Ryan did his best to sound chipper. "I'll go back in and get it."

She looked at him and winced. "You don't mind?"

"No problem. I'll be right back." He turned and fought his way against the crowd and back into the school.

Becka rolled her chair off to the side, out of the flow of people. She didn't need someone bumping into her and accidentally knocking her down the steps. Granted, the odds were slim, but after all that had gone wrong today, she didn't want to take anymore chances.

First there was Scotty's little wake-up call at three this morning. It took some work, but Becka had finally pried the information out of him. According to Kara, the curse was still on . . . which had reduced the chances of Becka getting back to sleep that morning to about zero.

Then there was the giant zit forming on the left side of her nose. But not just any zit, no sir. This was the queen mother of all zits. Tender and so red that, even under makeup, it was practically glowing.

Great, she'd thought as she stared at her reflection. *I'll be able to replace Rudolph this Christmas.*

"It's from all the stress," Mom had insisted. "I wouldn't worry about it."

Wouldn't worry about it? Obviously it had been a while since Mom had been in high school. But it wasn't the pimple that bothered Becka as much as it was the timing. She nervously reached up and touched it. *Pretty coincidental. They cast a spell on me, and I wind up in the* Guinness Book of World Records *for zits.*

Then there was Muttly. Of course, puppies make messes. But right on the carpet? Right in front of her room? Just before Ryan was to pick her up?

And let's not forget the spilled lunch tray at noon. Definitely one of her smoother moves. Chicken Cacciatore all over her jeans and new sweatshirt—the one she'd spent so much on to impress Ryan.

Everyone in the lunchroom had seen. Seen? They'd clapped. And of course, she'd turned your basic I'm-a-world-class-fool red. Ryan was immediately at her side. "You're just jumpy," he had assured her as he handed her some napkins. "Try to relax."

She had nodded, too embarrassed to look up, busying herself with scooping the food from her lap and back into the tray.

Then Ryan had suddenly exclaimed, "Becka, look at your hands. You're trembling. You're shaking like a leaf."

Becka had raised her hands and stared at them. *What's happening to me?* She'd bit her lip, then looked up to Ryan. Somehow she was able to hold back the tears, but inside . . . inside she was screaming. *Dear God, please make them stop! Whatever they're doing to me, make them stop!*

Now, outside in the front of the school, Rebecca took a deep breath and watched the kids head down the steps. Of course, Mom, Ryan, Scott, even Z would say she was bringing all this on herself with her own fears, her own nervousness. But she wasn't buying it. Not for a second.

She heard a voice call, "Excuse me? Rebecca?"

She looked over to the front doors. A couple of kids were pushing their way toward her. She guessed they were underclassmen, and they definitely were dressed like MORs.

Everyone at Crescent Bay High had their mode of dress: the surfers had their baggy shorts, the jocks had their T-shirts, the grungies had their plaids, the nerds had their hand-me-downs. Then there were the kids like herself, the MORs—Middle-of-the-Roaders. People who tried to stay in style but never went too far out on a limb, either because they couldn't afford it or because their folks wouldn't let them.

The two girls who now approached were definitely MORs.

"Are you Rebecca Williams?"

Becka nodded, figuring they already knew. After today, who wouldn't?

"I'm Jenny Fields," said the smaller of the two, smiling. She had long chestnut hair and a freshly scrubbed look about her. "And this is Kathy."

Becka tried to smile, but something inside was already telling her to be careful. "What's up?" she asked, clearing her throat.

"It's the weirdest thing," Jenny said as she reached into her jeans, "but my dad, he's, like, a pastor . . . anyway, he got a fax real late last night. And . . . uh . . ." She hesitated.

"And what?"

"Well, it was about you."

Becka felt herself stiffen. "Me?"

Jenny nodded. "The fax asked my dad to have me give this to you." She reached out her hand. In it was a slip of paper. Becka eyed it warily. "It's just the address of our church," Jenny assured her.

Becka took the paper and unfolded it. It read:

Community Christian Church
351 Cedar Road
Sunday Service, 11:00

Becka looked back up to her questioningly.

Jenny shrugged. "He just wanted us to let you know. Oh, and to tell you about our youth group. Tonight's pizza night. We're meeting around six."

Becka remained noncommittal. "Who did you say faxed your dad?"

"The guy, he didn't give his name. Just an initial."

Becka drew in her breath. She knew the answer before Jenny finished.

"He called himself Z."

Becka nodded.

"Do you know him?" Jenny asked.

Rebecca sighed, "We're old friends." A brief pause settled over the conversation as Becka looked back down to the note. She could feel Jenny's eyes searching her. Finally she looked up, managed a tight little smile, and said, "Thanks."

"No problem." Jenny grinned. Another pause. "Well, I, uh, I guess we'll see you around."

Becka nodded. The two girls turned and started down the steps. As they reached the bottom and disappeared into the crowd Becka looked back to the slip of paper. Her hands were trembling again. As they did, the paper slipped away and fluttered to the concrete.

She moaned in frustration. Was there no end to the day's irritations? She bent down to pick it up just as a gust of wind blew it further away, closer to the edge of the steps.

"Come on," Becka muttered as she grabbed one of her chair's wheels and rolled herself forward. She drew precariously close to the edge, but she would only be there a second. She reached down. The wind scooted the paper another half inch. She strained forward, jerking slightly, barely catching the paper's edge between her fingers.

What happened next Becka could never explain. Either it was her jerking forward, or someone had accidentally bumped into her chair, or . . .

Whatever the case, the right wheel slipped over the edge.

Becka immediately threw herself backward, trying to keep upright, but she was too late. Everything turned to slow motion as the wheel dropped, dragging the rest of the chair with it.

Becka knew she could not stop the fall, but she also knew she had to straighten out the chair. If she was going down the steps, she would have to face them head-on, otherwise the chair would twist sideways and she'd be thrown out.

She grabbed the left wheel and straightened it. She didn't scream. She had no time. She hit the first step, and as the chair pitched forward, she leaned back with all her might. Somehow she managed to keep the chair upright while fighting the wheels to keep it straight.

She hit the second step, then the third, the fourth—they were jarring, bone-rattling bounces, but she hung on—the fifth, sixth, seventh. She was going too fast. She had to break her speed. She squeezed the wheel rails with all her might and felt the heat sear into her palms . . . eighth, ninth, tenth . . . two more to go, two more and she'd make it . . . eleventh, twelfth, and finally she hit the sidewalk.

She quickly rolled to a stop. She was bruised, her palms were blistered, but she had made it. Of course, everyone stared. A few jerks thought it would be cute to applaud. But she barely had time to be embarrassed before Ryan burst through the doors and raced down the steps toward her. "Becka! Are you all right?"

She nodded and drew a deep, ragged breath. She looked down at her blistered hands. The shaking was worse now. Impossible to stop. So were the tears.

"What were you doing?" Ryan was shouting. Not in anger, but fear. "What were you trying to prove?"

She opened her mouth but nothing came.

"Becka? Rebecca." He reached out and took her hands, trying to stop the shaking. But he couldn't. It was then that they both noticed the crumpled slip of paper in her fist. She was still holding the address of the church.

Several blocks away, Scott was making his own exit. It was less dramatic than his sister's, but he still had plenty on his mind. Ever since Kara's phone call that morning, Becka had been in his thoughts. He'd even prayed for her. Was it just coincidence that all of these things were happening to her? Was it just Beck's nerves?

That hanging rat they'd found in her locker was definitely no coincidence. Rats just didn't crawl into your locker and hang themselves—or leave interesting notes. And what about the threats and those satanic ceremonies that were supposedly taking place? Didn't they count for something?

Earlier, he had tried to track down Brooke, the supposed leader. She was in the same grade as he was. But she wasn't in school. It seems she had been missing a lot of school these days. *Probably the late hours she's been keeping,* Scott scoffed.

"Scott . . . Scott, wait up."

He looked up to see Kara running toward him. He definitely appreciated the sight of her trim body, her thick red hair, those jade green eyes . . . yes sir, this girl was a breath stealer. And even though he was concerned about his sister, he wasn't too concerned to be flattered by Kara's interest.

"Hey, guy," she said, bouncing up to him.

"Hey, yourself," he said, trying to sound cool and in control. It would have worked, too, if his voice hadn't cracked.

"Is this a beautiful day or what?"

Scott looked around. He hadn't noticed before, but now that she mentioned it, she was right, it was beautiful. A crisp, clear day, with sure signs of spring just around the corner. "Yeah," he answered, grateful that his voice was momentarily in control, "it is pretty cool."

Kara closed her eyes. She tilted her face up to the sun and breathed in slow and deep. It was as if she was smelling the day, almost tasting its beauty. By the ecstasy on her face, maybe she was.

"You really get into it, don't you?" Scott chuckled.

She laughed with him, and the sound was as beautiful and carefree as she was. "I get into *everything,*" she said with a mischievous twinkle—and Scott suddenly wondered if she was talking about more than just the weather. He immediately looked away, feeling guilty for thinking such a thing.

Kara didn't seem to notice. "So how's your sister?"

"Not much better," he sighed.

"Yeah, Brooke can really be a jerk sometimes."

Scott stole a look in her direction. The sun reflected off the silver beads of her leather choker while highlighting her long, graceful neck, her determined chin, that cute little upturned nose. Scott seldom used the word *awesome*—he'd never really seen a reason for it . . . until now.

Still, he had to ask the question that had been on his mind ever since their meeting yesterday. He took a breath and began. "That's something I don't get," he said. "I mean, if you and Brooke are members of the Society and everything, why aren't you part of her little coven?"

"Satanists don't have covens. That's only for witches."

"Witches, satanists, whatever. What are you?"

"I'm . . ." She hesitated a second. "I prefer to call myself a pagan."

"A pagan?"

"Right," she said, tossing her hair aside, allowing the sun to sparkle off it like glittering copper. "Life is too sacred for us to go around sacrificing stuff. Besides, pagans don't believe in demons and Satan and devils and all that."

"What do you believe in?"

"Freedom. Freedom to do whatever I want. And Nature. I'm a big believer in Nature."

"Nature?" Scott looked at her, even more perplexed than before.

She laughed. "I believe everything is one, everything is interconnected. You, me—" she swooped down and picked up a nearby pinecone—"this pinecone . . . everything is the same. Everything is God."

"Everything is God," Scott repeated slowly to make sure he got it.

"That's right. The trick is to harmonize yourself with the natural forces around you and become part of that oneness."

"Welcome to California," Scott said, shaking his head.

"Don't laugh." She grinned. "It does have its advantages."

"Like what?"

"Well, if something feels good and it's Hnatural . . . I'll always do it."

There was that look again. That twinkle. Once again Scott glanced away, feeling both a rush of excitement and a stab of guilt. He stuck his hands into his coat pockets and tried to change the subject. "So, uh, how's your algebra coming?"

"That's what I wanted to talk to you about," she answered, as carefree and innocent as if nothing had passed between them. Maybe it hadn't. Maybe it was just Scott's imagination.

Come on, Williams, he told himself, *get your mind out of the gutter.*

Kara continued, "With midterms coming up next week, I'm going to need all the help I can get."

He nodded. "So, uh, when do you want to meet?"

Suddenly he felt both of her arms wrap around his as she moved in closer. It wasn't anything sexual. It was just Kara being her uninhibited, friendly self.

"How 'bout now?" she asked, looking up at him with that smile and those eyes. "How 'bout at your house?"

It may have been Kara being her uninhibited and friendly self, but she was definitely fogging up Scott's thinking. "Now?" His voice cracked again. "My house?"

"Sure, I mean if you're not doing anything."

"Um . . ." He was positive she had just said something . . . unfortunately he couldn't remember what it was. "Um . . ."

Come on, brain, work!

And then, somewhere in the back of his mind, another voice spoke.

Be careful.

It was barely discernible over all the emotion rushing through him, but it was definitely there. He cleared his throat. "My, uh, Mom won't be home till around six. Why don't you come by after dinner."

"You want me to come when your mom is there?" she asked in surprise. It almost sounded like ridicule. Immediately Scott hated himself for sounding so lame. Still, he remembered the rules he and Beck had agreed to months before: no guest of the opposite sex at the house without an adult. It wasn't that Mom didn't trust them, it was just . . . well, they all agreed it was just a good policy. Why put yourself in a risky situation if you didn't have to?

Of course, he still thought it was a good policy, but that didn't stop him from feeling like a fool. He quickly scrambled to come up with a better excuse. "I've got a lot of chores to do. You know, work in the garage and stuff." (He *had* promised to empty some of those stacked boxes.) "So, uh, later tonight—" His voice croaked again and he cleared it—"later would be a lot better."

"OK," Kara laughed as she removed her arms, "if you say so." Then, with that mischievous grin, she said, "We'll see you tonight." She turned and dashed across the street while Scott stood there, watching her go, feeling very much like he'd just been hit by a truck.

5

Shortly before six that evening, Rebecca and Ryan stopped in the doorway of the Community Christian Church's youth room. They were shocked at the destruction—ripped sofas, broken chairs, a smashed stereo, walls smeared with plenty of mud and who knows what else, and lots of black spray painted graffiti. A dozen high school kids were picking up the debris and scrubbing down the walls as an older, college-aged couple helped and gave instructions.

"You made it," Jenny, the girl who had invited Becka, called from across the room. She had just brought in some pizza boxes and was setting them on a table. She brushed her hands and headed toward them.

Coming here had been Becka's idea. She was grateful that Ryan was interested in church, but she would have come with or without him. The reason was simple. She was mad. Real mad. After recovering from "shooting the rapids" on the school steps that afternoon, she had finally made up her mind. She had told Scott her decision just a few hours earlier as he worked in the garage.

"I'm not going to be a victim anymore. We've beaten these guys twice already—you against that Ouija board and both of us against all the reincarnation junk. We can do it again. I know we can."

Scott had agreed as he lifted another box and moved it across the room. "They want a war," he said, "we'll give 'em a war."

Becka shook her head. "Not on our own, little brother. We need recruitments. You heard what Z said. We need to get plugged into a church."

"But where? Which one?"

Becka smiled as she unfolded the piece of paper with the address. "As usual, Z's looking out for us." She handed it to her brother, gave him a moment to look it over, then said, "I'm going to give Ryan a call to see if he wants to go. You want to come with?"

"I, uh, I'd like to. . . ." Scott hesitated, as though he was mulling something over. "But, Kara . . . she's coming over later this evening."

"So bring her along."

"I don't think so." Scott avoided her eyes.

"Why not?"

"I just don't think she'd fit in."

Becka watched him carefully. Something was up. Normally Scott was all overconfidence and wisecracks. Now he seemed nervous and cautious. She wanted to ask what was going on but figured he'd tell her when he was ready. She wheeled her chair out of the garage and into the kitchen, where she called Ryan.

That had been just a few hours ago. And now here they were, in the doorway of a church's youth room that looked like it had been struck by a hurricane.

Jenny came up to them, brushing stray wisps of hair from her face. "Sorry about the mess."

"What happened?" Ryan asked.

"We got hit pretty hard last night."

"Vandals?" Becka asked.

"Yeah," Jenny said, "or worse." She motioned toward the walls. "Take a look at that."

On one wall was spray painted the numerals *666*. Another wall sported drawings of lightning bolts. A third had a cross inside the universal no symbol, a circle with a slash through it.

"Not very friendly," Ryan said.

Jenny nodded. "We think they could be like satanists or something. A couple of the kids are pretty upset."

"What's that?" Becka asked, pointing to two lines of letters spray painted across the front wall. They read:

NEMANATAS

ACCEBERREDRUM

"We haven't figured it out," Jenny said with a shrug. "Probably some sort of code. The cemetery next door got hit, too. They knocked over a bunch of tombstones and dug up somebody's grave."

Ryan grimaced. "That's sick."

"Not only that, but they took the skull and—"

"Hi, guys." They were interrupted by the college-aged woman. She wasn't gorgeous by any stretch of the imagination, but there was something warm and genuine about her. Becka liked her instantly. "Who're your friends, Jenny?"

Jenny stepped back and made the intros. "This is Rebecca Williams and her friend . . ."

Ryan stepped forward and shook her hand. "Ryan, Ryan Riordan."

"I'm Susan Murdock," the woman said. "And that good-looking specimen over there—" she pointed to the man scooping up a pile of papers—"is my incredible husband, Todd."

Jenny laughed, "Newlyweds. They've been married all of six weeks, in case you can't tell." Everyone chuckled.

Jenny turned back to Susan. "Becka just moved up from South America. Her dad was a pilot who flew missionaries into jungle villages and stuff."

Becka stared at Jenny. Apparently the girl had gotten this information from Z. She frowned, wondering what else he had told her. Did he mention that Becka's dad had also died in one of those flights? That they had never found his body?

Before Becka could ask, Susan reached out and tapped the cast on her leg. "What happened here?"

Becka shook her head. "It's a long story."

"Who's your artist?" Ryan asked, motioning to the walls. Becka knew he was changing the subject for her, and as always, she was grateful for his sensitivity.

"Pretty sad, isn't it?" Susan sighed.

"Susan thinks she knows the kids," Jenny offered.

All eyes looked to Susan. She shrugged. "Well, one of them, yeah. Laura Henderson. I've been working with her for months. I guess this is her way of telling me to back off."

"Not very subtle," Ryan said, shaking his head.

Susan continued, "She's basically a good kid. Her home life's a mess, though. She's pretty desperate for some sort of control, something to hang on to."

"OK, everybody," Todd shouted to the room. "That's enough for now. Those of you who want to stick around and help afterward, great. But let's grab some pizza and get started."

"We'll talk later," Susan said as she started toward the front.

Jenny accompanied Ryan and Becka to the pizza table. Becka took a deep breath. She wasn't crazy about meeting new people. In fact, she hated it. But Z had suggested they do this, and so far Z had never been wrong.

Scott continued rummaging through the junk stacked in the garage. The previous tenants had left dozens of boxes behind, and it was his job to go through each and every one to see if there was anything worth saving. Some of the stuff was pretty strange—used toothbrushes, plastic milk cartons, the bottom half of tennis shoes. Yessir, whoever lived here before was definitely unique, in a *Ripley's Believe It or Not* sort of way.

Then, of course, there were the strange noises they'd heard in the garage, along with the eerie streaks of light that flew across the room. It's not that Mom and Becka were scared or anything—they were sure there was a logical explanation for it all. They just weren't crazy about being in the garage alone. So Scott, being the official man of the house, had been assigned the job of working there. He'd muttered something about sexism, but it did little good. He could mutter all he wanted. He still got the job.

But right now the noises and lights were not on his mind. Instead, he was thinking of red hair sparkling in sunlight, incredible green eyes, and a fun-loving smile.

He glanced at his watch for the hundredth time. He had done the right thing, putting Kara off till Mom got home. But the hours and minutes seemed to drag by. She was practically all he could think about. It's not that he hadn't seen beautiful girls before. Or never been attracted to them. But not like this. This one was special. And to top it off, this one was interested in him. Very interested.

What had she said? *"I'm a pagan. . . . I believe in freedom . . . if it feels good, I do it."* Scott forced the thoughts out of his mind. He took a deep breath and heaved another box onto the others. You didn't have to be a genius to know what she meant. You'd have to be deaf and blind not to know what she meant. Deaf and blind . . . and dead!

Scott sighed. For most of the guys at school, this would have been the opportunity of a lifetime. Something they dreamed about. But Scott knew what he should do: Cut her off. Don't get involved. Run from temptation.

But even as he thought that, he heard another voice: *Maybe I can help her. Maybe take her to church. Who knows, she might even—*

"Hey, guy."

He started, and immediately felt his heart begin to pound. "Hey, yourself," he said, turning toward her.

"Sorry I'm early." Her smile said she wasn't sorry in the least.

"No sweat," Scott replied, trying to stay nonchalant.

Suddenly, right on cue, there was a loud *SCREECH!*

Scott's eyes darted to the rafters. Fortunately it was bright enough in the garage that they couldn't see the darting light that always accompanied the sound.

"What is that?" Kara asked, stepping closer.

"Don't worry," Scott said, still staring at the rafters. "Just our pet ghost."

"No, really, what was that?"

"We're not sure."

SCREECH—SCRAPE.

"That's so weird." But instead of backing off, Kara moved in to investigate. "It sounded like it came from up there in the ceiling."

Before Scott could respond, she hopped up on some nearby boxes. Her impulsiveness didn't surprise him. Nothing she did surprised him anymore. She crawled to the next level of boxes, almost even with the bare bulb that hung down. Then she stood up, balancing herself precariously.

Scott didn't mean to stare. But even in the harsh light of the bulb she looked gorgeous. The flowing gauze skirt and unitard top didn't help matters. It was a struggle, but at last Scott forced himself to look away.

"Nothing here." Kara sounded disappointed.

"Hmm," Scott said, pretending to examine the contents of his latest box. Not that he knew what he was looking at. If it had been gold coins, he wouldn't have seen them.

"Aren't you going to help me down?"

Scott looked up. Kara stood on the box above him, holding out her hands. Somewhere in the back of his mind he heard, *Be careful,* but the voice was growing fainter by the second.

"Oh . . . uh, yeah. Sure." Scott fumbled to close the box lid and quickly moved to her aid. He reached up; she reached down. It was the first time their hands had touched since that afternoon. Then, before he could react, Kara placed his hands on her waist and gave a little hop. He had to move closer to catch her weight, and suddenly, as he lowered her, they were nice and close. Too close.

"Thanks," she said, shaking her hair back and gazing up at him.

Scott said nothing. He wasn't sure he could speak even if he wanted to.

Holding his gaze, Kara wrapped her arms around his neck, rose up on her toes, and brought her lips toward his. The voice in his head was screaming, but he paid little attention.

Until another voice broke in:

"Hey, Scotty. Who's your friend?"

Scott spun around. Mom was standing in the kitchen doorway. The look on her face showed surprise—and disappointment.

The youth meeting at the church was good. Becka had forgotten how much she missed being with other believers. Oh sure, some of them were just hangers-on, guys and girls scoping out each other, but there was a handful of kids who were really committed to God. You could tell by the way they got into the singing. The songs weren't just the fun, hand-clapping, I'm-glad-to-be-a-Christian-aren't-you type of stuff. There were also some worship tunes that were really directed to Jesus—songs that told him how much they loved him.

Becka didn't know many of the words (being stuck in remote South American jungles kind of keeps you from learning the latest hits). As the new kid with a non-Christian friend at her elbow, she was definitely on the self-conscious side. But eventually she was able to force that stuff out of her mind long enough to start worshiping a little herself. It felt good. Real good.

The teaching wasn't bad either. "The one

who is in you is greater than the one who is in the world." That was the Bible verse Todd kept referring to. He was obviously trying to comfort the kids who were upset and nervous about all the damage. He talked a lot about the authority Christians have over Satan . . . the promises Jesus made to Christians that they can stomp on the devil if they believe and use that authority.

But as Becka tried to concentrate on what he was saying, she kept being distracted by the writing scrawled across the wall behind him.

NEMANATAS

ACCEBERREDRUM

Maybe it's a foreign language, she thought. *Or initials. But why are the last two words in English?* Red rum. *Isn't booze usually clear or brown? Why* red? *Are they talking about blood?*

Becka tried to direct her attention back to Todd. Now he was talking about the need to love and forgive our enemies. He was explaining that most people involved in the occult are looking for love, that they're terribly insecure and searching for some sort of control in their life.

Becka really tried to concentrate. But her mind drifted again. *Maybe the words are*

English, but just mixed up. She examined the letters of the first word. Nema. *That could be . . .* name. *Or* men *with an extra* a *. . . or flip the* a *around and make* amen. Her eyes widened. That was it! *Nema* was a backwards *amen!* And if you read the second word backward you got—

Suddenly Becka went cold. She felt her body stiffen. Ryan looked at her. A slight frown crossed his face. As though he sensed her tension, he leaned over and whispered, "You all right?"

Becka swallowed hard and tried to remain calm. "Yeah, uh . . ."

Ryan looked at her carefully. "What's wrong?"

"I, uh . . ." Even at a whisper her voice was starting to quiver. "I think I know what those letters mean," she said, not taking her eyes from the front wall.

Ryan shot a glance to the wall, then back to Rebecca.

She continued staring straight ahead. "Remember . . . ," she whispered, "remember I told you that Scotty's friend said sometimes satanists speak backwards?"

"Yeah."

She closed her mouth. She wanted to say more, but she didn't trust her voice. She simply nodded toward the wall.

Ryan looked to the first line:

NEMANATAS

ACCEBERREDRUM

"Satan amen," he whispered. "The first line reads Satan, amen."

He looked at her and she managed to nod, but she couldn't take her eyes from the second line. He looked back at the wall and read:

NEMANATAS

ACCEBERREDRUM

"Mur derrebec ca." He scowled. "I don't get it."

Becka managed a hoarse whisper. "Say it faster." Her head was beginning to throb. "Say it faster."

"Mur derrebec ca . . . Murderrebecca . . . Murder rebecca." He gasped loudly, "Murder Rebecca?!"

"I'm sorry." Todd stopped his talk. "Did you have a question?"

Everyone turned to look at them. Rebecca stared down at her lap. Then she noticed it.

The shaking had returned. More violent than ever.

6

"All right," Mom said, shutting the front door and turning to Scott.

Uh-oh, he thought, *here it comes. . . .*

Mom had been pleasant enough to Kara for the few minutes the girl had remained. She'd asked Kara where she lived, what her interests were, would she like to stay for dinner. But Kara suddenly remembered something she had to do at home. She excused herself and was out the door in less than two minutes.

And now that Kara was gone, so was Mom's smile. "Looks like you've got some explaining to do, young man."

Scott figured he had two choices: either play the penitent sinner who promised never to break the rules again, or pretend to be outraged that his own mother didn't trust him. Unfortunately, he chose the latter. "Why do you always have to think the worst?" he accused.

"I come home to find you making out with a girl in the garage—what am I supposed to think?"

"We were not making out."

"You sure weren't finding a cure for world hunger!" Mom strode past him and headed into the kitchen. She'd had a long day of looking for work. He could tell she was cranky and hungry. And Muttly didn't help matters—the way he scampered around her feet, causing her to trip every few steps.

Scott followed her into the kitchen. "Kara's a nice girl. She just wanted some help in algebra."

"You know the rules, Scotty." Mom opened

the refrigerator, looking for something fast and easy to fix.

"So you don't trust me, is that it?" Scott demanded. Strategically speaking, he thought this was a good move, to keep Mom on the defense. But Mom had some pretty good moves of her own.

"I don't trust the world," she countered. She slammed the refrigerator and crossed the room to let Muttly out the back sliding-glass door.

"Maybe that's our trouble," he shot back. "Maybe the world knows a lot more than we give them credit for."

"And what is that supposed to mean?"

Scott wasn't entirely sure, but he'd already committed himself, so he couldn't back down. "This is the twenty-first century, Mom. California. But it's like we're living in a time warp." It surprised him to hear the anger in his own voice. "You've got me and Beck living in the Dark Ages."

"Right," Mom countered, both angry and hurt. "And this is one medieval mother who still grounds her kids for mouthing off."

"Fine," Scott snapped. He turned and stormed up the stairs toward his room. "Ground me for life! What difference does it make? I'm living in prison anyway!"

Mom followed him to the steps. "And you

think hanging out with that girl, doing whatever she wants—you think that's freedom?"

"I think she knows more about freedom than I'll ever know!" He stomped into his room and slammed the door. He stood there, breathing hard. He wasn't sure how the argument had gotten so out of hand. He believed what God said about honoring parents—and he believed what the Bible said about sex and stuff. But still . . .

"BEAM ME UP, SCOTTY, BEAM ME UP! *SQUAWK!* BEAM ME UP!"

He looked over at Cornelius, took another deep breath, and slowly let it out. How had everything gotten so crazy?

It was 8:55 P.M.

"Shine the light over there," Meaty Guy snarled.

His partner, Shaved Head, tried to ignore the sour smell of alcohol that hung on Meaty Guy's breath and snapped on the flashlight. He carefully ran the beam along the sagging back-alley fence. There had to be some sort of gate or opening. "You sure this is the place?" he whispered.

"Uh, 730 North Sycamore," Meaty Guy grumbled. "Two story, white with blue trim. This is it." They moved closer. The gravel of the alley crunched and popped under their feet. When they arrived at the fence Meaty Guy peered over it, searching. "There!" He spotted a rusting latch at the far end.

Shaved Head shined the light in that direction, but Meaty Guy angrily shoved it away. "Don't be stupid. They're home, can't you see?" He motioned toward the sliding-glass door, where Mom was clearing off the table after her dinner.

"Come on," Meaty Guy ordered. He adjusted the large shoe box under his arm and started for the gate.

"I think maybe Todd and Susan are right," Ryan said as he wheeled Becka from his car toward the open garage door. Since there were no ramps leading up the front porch, they had to enter and exit through the garage. "Maybe we should call the cops."

"And tell them what?" Becka asked. "That somebody's casting a spell on me?" She tried to sound strong, though she still hadn't been able to stop the trembling in her hands. "They won't believe it's real. Even you don't believe it."

Ryan pushed the hair out of his eyes. "I believe what's happening is real. I just don't think everything has to be supernatural."

They entered the garage. Since the kitchen door was only twenty feet away, Ryan didn't bother to snap on the light. "I can't buy that a bunch of losers can get together and suddenly have supernatural powers over you, that's all. Especially with what Todd was saying about God being greater."

"So I'm just being superstitious, is that it?" There was an edge to Becka's voice, which she immediately regretted.

Ryan chose his words carefully. "I just think . . . you're . . . giving them more credit than they deserve."

They had nearly reached the door when they were interrupted by a clear sounding *SCREECH—SCRAPE!* followed by a flash of light that darted across the room and disappeared out of sight.

Ryan and Becka froze. Becka glanced up to him and forced a grin. "So everything has to be logical and rational, huh?"

Ryan gave a weak, halfhearted smile and quickly moved them toward the kitchen door.

Muttly sat on the back porch, panting. Ever since Mom had let him outside, he had worn himself to exhaustion chasing leaves. Then his tail. And most recently, jumping into the air trying to snatch the moon out of the sky.

(Mongrel puppies have never been known for their outstanding intelligence.)

Suddenly, a hand reached over the fence toward the latch. Muttly cocked his head.

The hand grasped the latch and pulled it up. The gate swung open with a gentle groan. Muttly rose to his feet and gave a shiver of delight as two humans came into the backyard. From the way his tail wagged, it was plain he figured these were two new friends to play with.

The humans spotted him almost as quickly as he had spotted them.

"Perfect," the bigger of the two sneered. "We don't even have to look for him." Then, stooping down, he patted his leg and whispered, "Here, boy . . . come on, fellow . . . come on. . . ."

Muttly bounded off the porch and raced toward the beckoning human with eager anticipation.

"Come here, fellow, come on. . . ."

The pup was momentarily distracted by a wayward leaf that crossed his path. But soon his attention was back to the human who kept calling and motioning for him to come. The guy had pulled a box out from under his arm. "Come on, fellow. . . ." Now he was taking off the lid. "Come on. . . ."

Muttly was practically there. With two final

bounds, he reached the human, who suddenly scooped him into his arms. Muttly wriggled ecstatically.

Then the human stuffed him into the box and slammed the cover on top.

"Perfect," the guy sneered. "Just perfect."

Scott had just logged on to his computer. He'd heard Ryan's Mustang pull into the driveway and the slamming of the kitchen door as Ryan and Becka entered through the garage. Mom was taking a bath. He hoped it would be a long, hot one. She needed to relax. In the meantime, since it was nine o'clock, maybe Z would be on-line. He typed:

Hey, Z, are you there?

Good evening, New Kid. How was church?

I didn't go.

I know.

The answer didn't surprise Scott. The boy hesitated a moment. The two of them had been through a lot together. And through it all, Z had never betrayed his confidence. Maybe he could help here.

Z, you know I believe in the Bible and stuff. But . . .

He paused. After a moment Z typed:

But?

Scott took a breath and went for broke:

There's this girl. I mean she's so free and easygoing and . . .

Beautiful?

Well, yeah. And, uh . . . she's like really putting the moves on me and, uh . . .

Z interrupted:

She wants to have sex with you?

Scott raised his eyebrows and typed:

Yes.

What do you want?

That's just it. I mean, I believe the Bible. If it says sex before marriage is wrong, then it's wrong. But . . . times change—and, let's face it, the Bible was written a long time ago.

Scott waited. There was no reply.

Z, are you still there?

The words formed:

I'm gathering statistical data. Stand by.

Scott snorted and typed:

Z, I'm talking about my heart here,
not statistical data.

But Z paid little attention. Instead, the information quickly formed on the screen:

According to current reports, 75% of all AIDS transmissions now take place between males and females having sex. The biggest increase of AIDS cases is among teens.

Scott sighed. He already had the answer and typed:

Condoms.

Z's reply was just as fast:

Condoms fail 16% of the time in preventing pregnancy. That's 1 out of 6 times. Sometimes because of breaks or leakage. Sometimes because of manufacturer defects. A woman can only get pregnant a few days a year, but you can be infected with AIDS or other viruses every day of the year.

Scott was surprised, but Z had more:

Besides pregnancy and the danger of diseases,
premarital sex creates emotional damage.
Emotional damage?
The following is statistical information—
cold, hard, scientific evidence. Those who have
sex before marriage:
—have less happy marriages
—are more apt to divorce after marriage
—are more likely to commit adultery after
marriage
—enjoy sex less after they are married
You're telling me all this has been proven?
Through research, yes. I must sign off now.

But Scott had a final question:

Z, this girl, she calls herself a pagan.
Do you know what a pagan is?
Yes, but you do not want to know.
Try me.

The letters formed slowly:

A pagan is many things, but in this
context she means—

Suddenly the screen went haywire—numbers and letters appeared everywhere.

"Oh man . . . ," Scott groaned. He'd forgotten to turn off call waiting. Somebody else was calling in on the line, completely disrupting Z's transmission. Of course, Scott tried to bring the information back, but he had no success. And that's too bad. Because if he had succeeded, he would have seen the end of Z's transmission.

It consisted of only one word:

witch.

"Beck," Scott hollered from upstairs. "You've got a call."

Becka set the hot chocolate down on the kitchen table. She wheeled herself to the wall phone beside the cupboard and picked up the receiver.

"Hello?"

"We have him," the voice said.

Becka recognized it instantly. It was the same voice that had been threatening her. She threw a look to Ryan. "Who is this? . . . Who do you have?" Her tone immediately brought Ryan to her side.

The voice calmly answered, "Why, your stupid little mutt, of course."

Becka's eyes darted to the floor, searching for some sign of Muttly—any sign. Her voice shook, but she held her ground. "You're not fooling anybody," she bluffed. "My dog's right here."

"Oh, is he?"

Suddenly Becka heard yelping and squealing through the phone. It was Muttly. No doubt about it. And he was in pain.

"Stop it!" Becka shouted. "What are you doing to him? Stop it!"

The voice answered icily, "He's just the warm-up act, Williams. You're the real show. Better get ready 'cause you're on next."

"Who is this? Who are you?" Becka shouted. Muttly continued whining and barking in the background. "Who is this?"

"Red rum," the voice laughed. "Red rum, red rum, red rum."

"Who is this?!"

"Your destiny is mine." There was a click, followed by the dial tone.

7

They called the police. The officers were polite and friendly, but they had no hard evidence to go on—just a couple of prank phone calls and a missing puppy. When Becka hinted about people casting a spell on her, the officers pretended interest, but she could tell they were simply waiting for her to get back to "the facts." So after a half an hour of taking detailed notes and promising to talk to some of the kids in the Society, the police left.

For the next two hours, Scott, Mom, and Ryan did their best to calm Becka's nerves while combing the neighborhood for Muttly. On both accounts they failed. Becka was more jittery than ever, and no one had seen Muttly.

"Maybe we'll have better luck tomorrow," Ryan offered as they rolled into the garage.

"I wouldn't bet on it," Becka murmured.

"You want to come inside for some popcorn or something?" Mom offered.

"No," Ryan said, "I should be taking off."

"You sure?"

"Thanks, though." He glanced down at Becka, who looked worn and worried. "Listen, why don't I come back tomorrow and we can give it another try?"

Becka shook her head. "It won't do any good. They're too smart. We won't find him."

Ryan nodded. "I know. I was just looking for an excuse to stick by you through all this."

She looked up to him and forced a smile. What an incredible, sensitive guy this Ryan Riordan was. "Thanks," she said softly.

"If you need a reason to come over, I've got one," Scott said.

"Yeah, what's that?"

With a dramatic flair, Scott spun around to the dozens of unpacked boxes still in the garage. "These." He grinned as he stretched out his arms. "You can help me finish unpacking all of these stupid boxes."

Ryan shrugged. "Why not? It's as good an excuse as any. Besides, maybe we'll get down to the real cause of those noises and light."

"You don't believe in our little ghost?" Mom teased.

"Ryan doesn't believe in anything supernatural," Becka said. It was part truth, part jab.

"Not exactly," he corrected. "The stuff they said at the meeting tonight, you know, about Jesus and God, that made a lot of sense. I just don't believe that every time something goes wrong it's the work of the devil. I mean, there's plenty of creeps out there without him always having to get involved."

Becka glanced away. Ryan had taken this line from the beginning. Come to think of it, so had Z. What was it Z said? *"The only power they have is the power you give them through your fear"?*

Maybe. But how do you know? How do you know what are mind games and what are legitimate satanic attacks?

"Maybe it doesn't matter," Mom said, picking up the conversation exactly where they had left it the night before. It was Saturday afternoon, and all four had returned to the garage to chip away at the stacks of boxes. They weren't entirely sure why they wanted to work except, like Ryan had said, it gave them a chance to stick together. They still hadn't heard anything about Muttly, but Becka kept the cordless telephone nearby. Just in case.

"Maybe what doesn't matter?" Scott asked Mom as he tore open another box.

"Whether we're fighting spiritual wars or wars of the flesh," Mom answered.

"'Wars of the flesh'?" Ryan asked.

Becka explained, "You know, the stuff you want to do but know you shouldn't?"

"Like punching out the latest satanist," Scott quipped.

Becka continued more seriously, "Or lying or drinking or cheating or—"

"Or having sex outside of marriage," Mom said, throwing a too obvious look in Scott's direction. Scott immediately looked down, pretending he hadn't heard.

Mom continued, "The point is, Jesus not only promised to give us victory over evil spirits, but also over our own flesh. All we have to do is pray and believe."

"So you agree with Ryan and Z?" Becka asked. "That these kids have no real power over me? That I'm just being stupid and superstitious?"

Mom hesitated. "I'm not sure, honey."

"I bet Muttly is sure," Becka grumbled. Her tone was sharp and Mom winced. But before Becka could apologize . . .

SCRAPE.

Everyone froze. There was no mistaking the sound. As usual it came from overhead. All eyes moved to the rafters, searching. Everyone stood in silence. Everyone but Scott.

"Casper?" he called. "Casper, is that you?"

"Shhh!" Becka motioned for him to be quiet.

If any of them had been alone, they would have moved for cover. But as a group they seemed to have more courage, so they held their ground. Their heart rates may have picked up, but they held their ground. At least for the moment.

SCRAPE.

Scott fidgeted. "All in favor of getting out of here, say aye!"

There were no answers. Lots of dry mouths and nervous coughs, but no answers.

SCRAPE.

Ryan was the first to spot it. "There!" he shouted and pointed. "Up there."

"I don't see anything," Scott said.

"It was a light. I only caught a glimpse of it, but it was a light. Right there." He started to climb onto one of the boxes. It crushed under his weight. He found another and crawled onto it.

"Ryan," Becka protested. But it did little good. He was already on a second box, then a third.

"I'm sure I saw it . . . right there." He grabbed another box and set it on top of his pile to get closer to the ceiling.

"Ryan," Mom said in her I'm-the-adult-here-so-you'd-better-listen-to-me voice, "be careful."

It was the fifth box that did it. Ryan's homemade mountain was not that stable, and suddenly everything began to lean.

"Watch it!" Scott called.

SCRAPE.

Whether it was the noise or Ryan's reaction to the noise, no one knew. But suddenly the entire pile of boxes toppled.

"Ryan!"

He fell hard and was immediately covered by boxes.

"Ryan! Ryan, are you OK?"

Mom and Scott dug through the boxes and finally pulled him out.

"I saw it," he said as they helped him to his

feet. "I saw sunlight." Then without hesitation he motioned to the mound of fallen boxes. "Scotty, hand those to me."

"Ryan, don't be stupid," Becka warned.

But he didn't listen.

"Ryan, we don't want you getting hurt," Mom insisted.

"I'll be fine," he said as Scott began handing him the boxes.

Soon they had rebuilt his mountain—more carefully this time. Much more carefully. Everyone watched as Ryan climbed the boxes. At last, Ryan reached the ceiling. He could actually touch the dilapidated plywood and rafters of the roof. He began to poke and feel and explore.

Everyone waited.

And then he chuckled.

SCRAPE.

"Ryan, are you OK?" Mom called.

The sound repeated itself again. *SCRAPE.* And again. *SCRAPE, SCRAPE.*

"What's going on?" Becka shouted.

Scott joined in. "Ryan, are you doing that?"

Ryan laughed again. His right arm was stretched through the rafters in the roof. He seemed to be spinning something.

"It's a ventilator," he shouted.

"A what?"

"One of those vents for the attic. You know, those aluminum balls on the roofs that spin round and around?"

"No way," Scott scoffed.

"Only this one's a little stuck so it takes quite a gust of wind to make her turn." To prove his point, he tugged harder with his arm, forcing the sound to repeat itself faster and faster: *SCRAPE-SCRAPE-SCRAPE-SCRAPE. . . .*

The Williamses grew silent, feeling a little foolish and a lot relieved.

Becka was the first to speak. "But . . . what about the light?"

"What about it? It's sunlight."

"What about at night, when there is no sun?"

"Got me," came the answer.

"Unless . . ." Now it was Scott's turn to smile.

Mom and Becka looked at him. "Unless what?" Mom asked.

"There's a streetlight in front of the house, right?"

"Yes. . . ."

Ryan completed the thought. "So on gusty nights, when this thing moves, the light reflects through the hole here and—"

"We have flying lights," Becka finished flatly.

"Bingo!" Ryan grinned.

Mom shook her head. "So much for our garage ghost."

"Well," Scott said with a shrug, "it was fun while it lasted."

Ryan gave the ventilator a few more spins—*SCRAPE-SCRAPE-SCRAPE*—and then started down, just as the phone rang.

Becka froze. Everyone exchanged glances. There was no chance for a second ring before Becka lifted the receiver.

"Hello?" But it was neither the police nor the icy voice. "Hi, this is Kara. Is Scott around?"

"Yeah, hang on." Rebecca held out the phone to her brother. "It's your friend Kara."

"Oh," Scott said, fumbling for the phone. "Uh, hello?"

Mom and Becka exchanged uncertain looks as Scott began to talk. There was something about the way he stammered and fidgeted that made them realize the boy was definitely smitten.

Scott edged out of the garage and into the kitchen, making it clear that he wanted his privacy. Mom looked after him. Try as she might, she couldn't shake the uneasiness welling up inside her.

She would have felt even more uneasy if she had known what Kara was asking.

~

"I still say we should have brought the van," Laura complained as she tossed the strands of rope into the trunk of her Nissan. "No way can we get her wheelchair in here."

"Don't be stupid," Brooke snapped. "She won't need a wheelchair where we're going."

The others snickered. Brooke saw Laura's face redden. She knew the girl hated being ridiculed, especially by her, especially in front of the group. Good. This would make Laura work all the harder. And that was good.

Brooke looked to the sky. It was almost sunset. Tree branches had started to stir. A mass of heavy black clouds approached. "Looks like a storm," she said with grim satisfaction. "You guys don't mind a little rain, do you?"

The six kids voiced their approval as they gathered around the Nissan and a VW Bug.

"What about the brother?" It was Frail Girl, the one who had vomited at the cemetery.

Brooke gave a sly smile. "I just got off the phone with Kara. Little brother is all taken care of."

"And Williams's boyfriend?" Laura asked.

Meaty Guy tossed a sawed-off baseball bat

into the back of the Nissan. "I can handle him."

Brooke eyed Meaty Guy. Like Laura, there was something about his anger and energy she liked. As long as he knew who was in charge, he would prove very useful. She turned to the rest of the group. "We've got the robes?"

"Check," Frail Girl said.

"Candles and incense?"

"Got 'em."

"Athamés?"

"Oh, yeah," Shaved Head chuckled nervously as he produced half a dozen small daggers.

"Nightgown?"

"Right here," Laura called, raising a white nightgown above her head.

"Ropes and gag?"

"We've got everything," Meaty Guy grumbled. "Let's get started."

"Not until sunset," Brooke insisted. "The powers of darkness do their best work in the dark." Then, looking around, she snapped, "The mutt. Who's got the mutt?"

Shaved Head grimaced. "Be right back." He ducked into the nearby trailer home and a moment later reappeared with a squirming pillowcase full of puppy.

"Put him in the VW," Brooke ordered.

Shaved Head nodded, opened the VW's door, and threw the bag in the back. It hit the floorboard with a sickening thud. For the moment, all movement inside the pillowcase ceased.

As Shaved Head slammed the door, Meaty Guy repeated, "Let's go. We can wait outside the house till it gets dark. Come on."

Brooke glanced to the rest of the group. They were primed, ready for action. She could feel their power, their anger waiting to be unleashed. This was good. Very, very good.

"OK." She nodded. "Let's do it."

They climbed into the cars. "Give me the keys," Meaty Guy said to Laura. "Let me drive."

Laura hesitated. The Nissan was her car.

"Let him have 'em," Brooke ordered as she climbed into the back.

"But—"

"Give him the keys."

Without further argument, Laura handed them over. She had been ridiculed by Brooke once this evening. That was more than enough.

Brooke, Shaved Head, Meaty Guy, and Laura rode in the Nissan. Frail Girl and her partner were in the VW.

Brooke rolled down the window and

shouted, "Make sure you've got it all set up by the time we get there!"

The two girls in the VW nodded and took off. Meaty Guy followed.

8

s 7:30 approached, Scott grew more and more anxious. It wasn't because Ryan was staying over for dinner. And it wasn't because the guy kept asking all sorts of cool questions about Jesus.

Scott was nervous because of Kara's phone call earlier that afternoon. She had asked if he'd come over around 7:30 to help her with her algebra. Not a major problem except, for some reason, Scott had not gotten around to telling Mom about it. He wasn't sure why. Maybe it had something to do with the little incident between them in the garage last night. Maybe it was because, in the back of his mind, he suspected Kara really wasn't that interested in mathematics.

Don't be stupid, he argued with himself. *You're letting your imagination run away with you again. She just wants help, that's all.* But if he really believed that, why wouldn't he tell Mom? He wasn't sure. The only thing he was sure about was that, the closer it got to 7:30, the harder it was to concentrate on the dinner conversation. And that was a pity because, as conversations go, it wasn't bad.

"I believe Jesus was a good guy," Ryan was saying, "one of our greatest teachers."

"Not exactly," Mom answered as she dished out a second helping of corn and passed it on to him.

"What do you mean?"

"Jesus couldn't be a great teacher."

Ryan looked surprised. "Why not?"

"Great teachers don't claim to be God."

"Jesus claimed that?"

"Over and over again. 'I am the way and the truth and the life,' 'I and the Father are one,' 'Anyone who has seen me has seen the Father.' Those are all claims he made about himself in the Bible."

Ryan glanced to Becka, who nodded in confirmation.

Mom continued, "No good teacher would make those claims about himself. A fruit-cake, maybe. Or some sort of con artist. But no good teacher would claim to be God."

"Unless—" Becka cleared her throat—"unless he really was God." It had been a while since Rebecca had talked to anyone about her faith, but Ryan was so open and interested that it just came naturally. She continued, "All the other so-called spiritual teachers, all they talk about is how to get rid of our sins through reincarnation or TM or whatever. But Jesus, he kept saying, 'I'm going to the cross to pay for those sins. Dump your sins on me; I'm going to die and take the punishment for you.'"

"So you're saying his death was no accident?" Ryan asked.

"That's right. Dying on the cross was his main reason for coming."

Ryan's next question came just a little bit slower. "And what exactly is our end of the deal? What are we supposed to do?"

"Just ask."

"Ask what?"

"Ask Jesus to take your punishment. Believe that he died on the cross for you."

Ryan looked at Becka skeptically. "That's it?"

"That's it." She held his gaze, feeling more confident than she had in days. "That's why he came and died—to take our punishment."

Ryan looked down and shook his head in quiet amazement.

"But there's a price," Mom added.

Ryan looked up.

"You have to let him be your boss . . . your Lord."

A brief scowl crossed Ryan's face—but it wasn't from anger, or even from concern—it was from thinking. Deep, earnest thinking.

The conversation continued, but Scott barely heard. He fidgeted nervously and gave another glance at his watch. 7:10. He looked back up just in time to meet his sister's eyes.

"You OK, Scotty?" she asked. She could read him like a book. Sometimes that was good. Sometimes, like tonight, it was lousy.

He did his best to cover with a smile and a shrug. "I promised to meet a friend at 7:30."

"Darryl?" she asked, her eyes still searching. "I haven't seen him around for a while. Not that I'm complaining, you understand. . . ."

Scott forced a chuckle. "Yeah, well he's been swamped studying for midterms. I thought I'd go over and give him a hand." Scott wasn't sure how the lie slipped in—he hadn't planned on it; it just came. And so did the guilt. He had to get out of there. He had to leave. He pushed himself from the table and stood.

"You're going to do homework on a Saturday night?" Mom asked skeptically.

"Oh, I'm sure we'll squeeze in a couple videos along the way." He forced another smile.

Mom returned it, not entirely convinced. "There's supposed to be a storm tonight," she said, watching him head toward the door. "Take your coat."

Scott nodded. He could feel their eyes on him as he grabbed his jacket from the coatrack and slipped it on. "You guys take care."

"You too," Ryan offered.

Scott opened the kitchen door and headed out. He didn't know why he was in such a hurry. It only took a few minutes to get to Kara's. Maybe it was the guilt he felt closing in around him. Maybe it was Becka's questioning eyes. Or maybe it was because the very stuff they were talking to Ryan about was stuff he believed—but right now it was stuff he was trying to push out of his mind. At least for tonight.

He headed down the driveway and started up the sidewalk. Dark billowing clouds hid the last traces of daylight. The storm would be there soon. He felt no better out here than he had inside at the table. In fact, he felt worse. And by the time he crossed the street at the end of the block, he was so preoccupied that he barely saw the speeding Nissan squeal around the corner and swerve wide to miss him. Of course the car honked and the kids inside swore, but Scott barely noticed.

He had more important things on his mind.

ϟ

The Nissan raced past Scotty, then came to a stop . . . directly across from the Williams house.

Here they turned off their ignition.

Here they waited for the dark.

ϟ

"You've sure given me a lot to think about," Ryan said as he wheeled Becka down the driveway toward his Mustang. They had sat around the table continuing their talk about Jesus—about the life he promised to give, the love he promised to deliver, and the peace he promised to provide. But when Mom and Becka asked if he was interested in that type of life, if he'd like to pray to receive Christ, Ryan had said no.

"It's a big decision," he had explained. "Especially the part about letting him be my boss. If I do it, I don't want to do it halfway. I've seen enough of those type of Christians running around."

The guy had a point. And Mom and Becka agreed that it was better for him to do a little research on his own, to "count the cost," instead of just blindly jumping in. So Mom had dug up a New Testament and suggested he give it a read. He took it and promised he would.

Now Ryan and Becka were calling it a day as they headed down the driveway toward his car. The storm was closing in. Wind was already beginning to blow against their faces and clothes. Although the sun had set, it was still possible to see the clouds churning and roiling above them. Suddenly there was a flash of lightning.

"Looks like it's going to be a big one," Ryan said, staring up at the sky.

The thunder followed, seeming to boom and roll forever. Becka folded her arms against the cold. "You want to stay until it blows over?"

"Nah, if I hurry I'll be able to outrun it." But even as he spoke fat raindrops started to splash on the driveway around them.

There was another flash, followed by an even closer clap of thunder.

They reached the car. Ryan dropped the Bible through the open passenger's window. Then, without a word, he kneeled down and took both of Becka's hands into his. As his deep blue eyes met hers, she instinctively knew what was next. It was something she longed for, something she dreamed about—but she knew the timing wasn't right. Not yet. The rain fell harder. He closed his eyes and leaned toward her. The temptation was overwhelming, but somehow Becka was able to find the strength. She gently put her fingers to his lips.

"No, Ryan. . . ."

He opened his eyes.

She shook her head and said softly, "I'm sorry."

He searched her face, a little surprised, but she saw understanding, not hurt, in those incredible blue eyes.

They continued to hold each other's gaze, the rain splattering on their faces and hair. At last, Becka reached up and brushed one of the rain-soaked curls from Ryan's eyes. "You'd better be going," she whispered.

"Yeah," he whispered back. But neither moved. The rain was pouring now.

Then they heard it. The creak and groan of an old car door. Ryan looked up. Across the street he saw a beat-up Nissan with all four of its doors opening. He thought it weird to see four people stepping out into this deluge. Weirder still that they were all heading toward him.

"Hey, Ryan," the biggest of the group shouted over the rain. "Can we talk to you?"

Ryan peered at them over his car. He could tell they were his age, maybe a little younger. But it was hard to recognize them through the rain. "Do I know you?" he called.

They crossed the street and rounded his car. Two guys and two girls. They stepped up on the curb. The biggest was holding something behind his back and smiling.

Ryan eyed them carefully. "What's going on?" he yelled over the pounding rain. His voice carried an edge—not unfriendly, but definitely demanding.

"It's my car," the big guy shouted. "Battery's dead. Can you give me a jump?"

Ryan didn't believe him for a second. Why would all four kids pile out into this pouring rain to ask for a jump?

"Ryan?" It was Becka. He recognized her

tone instantly. It was thin and wavy, like the other times she had been frightened.

He was torn. He did not want to take his eyes off the others, especially the big guy. Yet he knew Becka was scared and needed assurance. It was against his better judgment, but he turned from the group for the slightest second and looked down to her. Before he could say a word, he saw her eyes widen in horror, her mouth opening to scream.

Ryan spun around just as the baseball bat smashed into his chest. For a moment he felt no pain, though the blow was hard enough to send him staggering. Before he could regain his balance, the big guy moved in with another swing. This time Ryan was able to raise his arm, trying to deflect the bat, but it still hit its mark, smashing into his forehead.

The pain arrived. Exploding. Searing.

Ryan heard Becka scream. But it was a distant scream, far away. The lightning flashed as the bat delivered its third and final blow, catching him on his right shoulder. Ryan barely felt this one. It was the second hit that had done the real damage.

He squinted, trying in vain to clear his vision. He felt something warm and wet flowing down his face. He hoped it was rain. He had his doubts. He heard another crash of thunder, directly above them now. At the same time, he felt his legs turning to rubber. Suddenly they gave way as he crumpled onto the wet pavement.

The laughter and screams were from another world now. Barely audible. He could hear some sort of scuffle, but try as he might, he could not make his body move to help. With excruciating effort, he turned his head. The wet concrete felt good against his burning face. As the lightning flashed, Ryan caught sight of Becka in a nightmarish, strobing light as she fought and screamed while they yanked her from her wheelchair.

And then he saw nothing.

"Hey, guy."

Scott stood in the doorway, dripping wet, looking and feeling very much like a drowned rat. But he no longer cared. For there, inside, stood a smiling Kara. She looked more attractive than ever. Maybe it was the thin silk blouse, or the way the candles from the living room glowed and flickered behind her. Whatever the reason, it was all he could do to croak out the expected "Hey, yourself."

"Looks like you got a little wet." She flashed him her grin and opened the door wider. He sloshed in. As she shut the door, he stood a moment, dripping on the entryway tile, taking it all in. There were no lights. Just the candles. Burning candles on the coffee table, the piano, the bookshelves, the entertainment center. Everywhere.

"I'll grab you some towels," Kara said, turning and heading for a hall closet.

"Guess you're saving on electricity," Scott tried to joke, but his cracking voice betrayed his uneasiness.

Kara disappeared around the corner and down a hall. "I think candles are a lot more romantic than regular light, don't you?"

"As long as your folks don't mind."

"My folks?" She reemerged with an armload of towels. "Didn't I tell you?"

"Tell me what?"

"My folks are out of town for the weekend."

9

"Ryan? Ryan, can you hear me?" The voice was muffled and far away. "Ryan . . ." But coming closer and slipping into focus. "Ryan, can you hear me?"

He began to feel the rain—wonderful, soothing rain—washing over his face, cooling the fire on his head. With it came other feelings, less welcome: the throbbing inside his brain, the ache of his shoulder, the stabbing pain in his chest.

"Ryan . . ."

The voice was louder now, clearer. He tried to open his eyes, but they were too heavy. They rolled but remained shut. He tried again and kept trying until, at last, they fluttered open.

He blinked rapidly against the splattering rain and saw Becka's mom staring down at him. At least he thought it was Becka's mom—she looked a lot different with her hair wet and plastered against her face. She was kneeling over him, holding his head. "Ryan . . ."

Lightning flashed behind her. He tried to move, but the pain in his chest was such a surprise that he gasped.

"Don't move, hon. You're hurt real bad."

But Ryan had to move. He had to see. He braced himself for the pain and sat up. The pounding in his head was excruciating, but he steeled himself against it. Breathing hard and ignoring the pain as best he could, he looked around. Then he spotted the empty, overturned wheelchair.

"Where is she?" His words came out in ragged gasps.

"I don't know. I heard the screams, but by the time I got outside they were gone."

"We've got—" He broke off, still struggling to breathe. "We've got . . . to follow them." He tried to get to his knees, but the pain exploded through his entire body. It was all he could do to hold back a scream.

"Easy now, stay there. Don't—"

"No!" He moved again. The edges of his vision grew white and blurry. He knew he was on the edge of blacking out. He used all of his concentration to hang on. He made it to his knees.

"Ryan . . ."

With Mrs. Williams's help he slowly rose to his feet. His legs were unsteady, but with her support he was able to lean against the car. Everything around started to spin, but he drew slow, even breaths until the movement stopped.

"Ryan, we've got to get you to a hospital."

"Call the police," he gasped. "Tell them to look for a brown, four-door Nissan."

"But what about—"

"We can take care of me later."

Mrs. Williams was torn. "But—"

"I'll be OK!" he shouted. The extra energy almost did him in. "Hurry!"

Still torn, Mrs. Williams released Ryan, making sure he was stable against the car.

"Hurry!"

His anger overcame the last of her hesitation. She turned and dashed through the rain toward the front door.

Ryan leaned against the car, gasping and wincing, waiting until she was out of sight. Then, using the car for support, he dragged himself around to the driver's side. By now it was impossible to distinguish between the burning in his chest, the ache in his shoulder, and the pounding in his head. It was all the same. Everything screamed at him.

But Becka had to be found. The Society had to be stopped. And soon. Becka's mom would only slow things down by insisting he go to the hospital. There was no time. He pulled open the door and tumbled into the seat. Pain forced a muffled cry to his throat, but he swallowed it back.

More lightning—a series, one flash after another after another.

He dug out his keys and righted himself behind the wheel.

Now what? Who knew where these kids lived, where they might go? His mind raced. Didn't Scott have a friend from the Society? That Kara girl? She'd know! But where does she live? What was her phone number?

Ask Scott. Yes!

No! Scott wasn't there!

Ryan slammed the wheel in frustration, sending another jolt of pain through his body.

Where was Scott? Where did he say he was going? To help some kid with his homework? Yes! His little dorky friend, Darryl!

Ryan put the key in the ignition and fired up the car. He had taken Darryl home after Becka's welcome-home party from the hospital. He knew exactly where the kid lived. He dropped the Mustang into gear and stomped on the accelerator. The wheels spun against the pavement, caught hold, then thrust the car forward.

He did not hear Mom as she raced out of the house, crying, "Ryan! Ryan, *no!*"

Becka fought and screamed until they shoved the gag into her mouth—so deep she thought she would choke. Then they taped it.

"Now her arms," Brooke ordered.

Laura pushed Becka's face against the back of the seat and cinched her hands. Becka cried out as the girl yanked on the rope, pinching and burning her wrists. But it was a cry no one heard. Besides the gag, there was the noise—the heavy-metal band in the tape deck, the water splashing under the racing car, the rain pounding on its roof.

There was another burst of lightning. Becka caught only flickering glimpses of rooftops and trees. She had no idea where they were.

The car reeked of alcohol as cans and bottles were passed back and forth.

Suddenly her hair was yanked hard until she was looking, face-to-face, at the chunky brunette leader. "So you think you're better than the rest of us?" Brooke demanded. "You think you've got more power than me?"

Rebecca couldn't have answered even if she hadn't been gagged. She was too petrified. All she could do was stare back at Brooke in wide-eyed horror.

Brooke laughed. "A little frightened, are we? Well, just hang on, Princess, 'cause you ain't seen nothing yet."

Becka was in a panic. She couldn't think, she couldn't plan. She tried desperately to regain control, but it did no good. What was it Z had said? *"The only power they have is the power you give them through your fear"?* If that was the case, then they had her lock, stock, and barrel. Big time.

And there was nothing she could do about it.

Ryan banged on the screen door a second time. There was still no answer. But someone was home—he could see the lights and hear the stereo. He banged a third time, even harder. The pounding sent shock waves through his body.

At last he saw movement behind the curtains. Darryl finally opened the door and peered into the darkness. "Ryan?" his voice squeaked. "You look terrible."

"I've got to talk to Scott."

"Scott Williams?" Darryl gave a loud sniff. "He's not here."

"Where'd he go?"

"How should I know? I haven't seen him all day."

Ryan scowled. "He said he was coming over here—to help you with your homework."

"On a Saturday night? You've got to be kidding."

Ryan wished he was. He closed his eyes and tried to keep his voice calm and even. "So Scott never showed here?"

"No." Darryl was staring at the gash on his forehead. "You want to come in, get that cleaned up?"

Ryan shook his head. "I've got to find Scott." He turned and headed down the porch steps, back out into the rain.

"What's going on?" Darryl called. "If I see him, what should I tell him?"

Ryan reached his car and opened the

door. "Just tell him to get home!" he shouted over the storm. "Tell him his sister needs him." Without waiting for an answer, he climbed behind the wheel, started up the Mustang, and took off down the road.

Now what?

He wasn't sure.

Where to?

He had no idea.

If he could just stop the throbbing in his head, maybe he could think. The rain continued to pour, and fog was forming on the inside of his windshield faster than the defroster could clear it.

He glanced to the seat beside him for a rag, anything to clear it off. To his surprise, he saw the New Testament Becka's mom had given him after dinner. An idea came to him. He threw the wheel to the left, and the car went into a skidding U-turn. He straightened it out and headed in the opposite direction—toward the Community Christian Church.

Laura Henderson's Nissan slid to a stop in the mud beside the VW. They were at the park.

Brooke was the first out of the car. "Strip her," she shouted. "Get her changed and take her to the altar."

Laura pulled Becka out of the car—the booze making her rougher and more eager to please Brooke than ever. Rebecca went completely out of control. Oblivious to any pain, she kicked and thrashed until suddenly she and Laura went down in the mud.

Laura swore as she yanked Becka to her feet and shoved her hard against the car. Frail Girl had seen the struggle and moved to help. Rebecca was whimpering now, sobbing hysterically. Laura grabbed the bottom of Becka's sweatshirt and started to peel it up over her head. Another wave of panic hit Becka, and she went crazy again, kicking and fighting for all she was worth.

"Stop it!" Frail Girl slurred. "Stop fighting us! You're only making it worse. Stop it! Stop it!"

But Becka didn't hear. She couldn't hear. She was raw terror, squirming and kicking and screaming . . . until Laura slapped her hard across the face. Becka barely noticed. Laura slapped her again. And again. Until Becka's struggling finally slowed to a stop.

Rebecca stayed hunched over the car, breathing hard. The slaps had done the trick. She was back in control. And with the control came the realization: *I haven't even prayed! How could I be so stupid?* The panic and fear had completely blotted God from her mind. But not now. She took another breath to steady herself, and finally she began to pray. *Jesus, help me, Jesus show me what to do, Jesus . . .*

As Becka prayed, Laura resumed peeling off her sweatshirt. Becka shivered as the rain hit her bare skin.

Jesus, Jesus, help me, help me. . . .

Laura got the sweatshirt over Becka's head, then swore again.

"What's the matter?" Frail Girl asked.

"Her hands are tied—we can't get the thing off."

"Should we untie her?"

"Nah, just give me the nightgown. No one will care."

Frail Girl reached into the car and handed Laura the white nightgown. "What about her pants?"

Jesus . . . please, no, Jesus. . . . Help me, help me. . . .

Laura gave a dubious look at the cast on Becka's leg. "Just throw the nightgown over her. What difference does it make?"

Becka sucked in her breath. It was a small victory, but it was enough. Z had said the only power they had was through her fear—nothing supernatural, just her fear. If that was the case, she had just proven him right. By refusing to give them her fear, she had been able to pray . . . and by praying, she had won a tiny victory.

Thank you, Jesus . . . thank you. . . .

They pulled her sweatshirt back down, then forced the nightgown over her head and onto her body. It formed a type of straitjacket, keeping her arms pinned to her sides.

"Come on," Laura ordered.

They half-walked, half-dragged Becka toward the woods.

Jesus, help me, show me what to do. . . .

The rain slowed to a stop, but only for a moment.

They rounded the bushes and entered the secluded spot, the one sheltered by a canopy of trees and impossible to see from the road. At its center was a picnic table. Four hooded figures stood around it. They held large flickering candles that were almost blowing out in the wind. On the ground surrounding them was a white circle of rope exactly nine feet across.

Sitting at the center of the table was a stained pillowcase with something moving inside. Scattered around it were more candles, some sticks of burning incense, a wine goblet, and several little daggers. Directly in front of the pillowcase was a large blazing candle stuck on top of a human skull.

Becka felt the fear returning, the loss of control. *NO! Please, Jesus . . . help me!*

One of the hooded figures stepped forward. "Welcome, Rebecca Williams." Becka couldn't see her face, but she instantly recognized Brooke's voice. "You have dared to challenge our powers, and it is time you pay the price. Your destiny belongs to me." She turned to another figure beside the picnic table and nodded. The figure reached for a silver dinner bell and rang it.

"Let the mass begin."

One of the figures pulled a card from her robed sleeve and began to read: "Amen. Forever glory the and power the and kingdom the is thine for."

Others from around the table fumbled with their cards and joined her: "Evil from us deliver but, temptation into not us lead."

As they continued, Brooke crossed to the makeshift altar. The rain had started again, but the group paid no attention. The more they read, the louder their chant grew. And the louder the chant grew, the more focused they became on the words—the more detached they became from reality.

"Debtors our forgive we as debts our us forgive and bread daily our day this us give."

Brooke reached for the goblet. Next she reached for one of the daggers on the altar.

She pulled up her left sleeve. The blade glimmered in the candlelight. All eyes were riveted on her arm. She hesitated the slightest moment, then dragged the blade over the back of her arm, slicing it deeply.

Rebecca gasped as the blood oozed. Her panic was nearly overpowering. She could barely hold it back.

Help me, Jesus, help me. . . .

"Heaven in is it as earth on done be will thy come kingdom thy."

Brooke reached for the wine goblet.

"Name thy be hallowed, heaven in art who father our."

Making a fist and flexing her arm, Brooke forced the blood to flow faster . . . until two, three, four drops fell into the bottom of the goblet.

Then, with a grin, she passed the goblet to the next figure, who was pulling up his own sleeve, reaching for his own dagger . . . as the group repeated the chant.

"Amen. Forever glory the and power the and kingdom the is thine for. . . ."

10

Ryan gunned his car until it skidded into the church parking lot. He pulled himself out of the car, then staggered to the sanctuary, where he threw open the doors and entered.

Susan Murdock, the youth worker he'd met last night, spun around in surprise. She'd been cleaning and preparing the sanctuary for tomorrow's service. Her voice was firm, but there was no missing her alarm as she squinted to the back of the church. "Who is it? What are you doing here? The church is not—" And then she recognized him. "Ryan?"

He stepped to the back pew and leaned against it for support.

Susan started toward him, walking, then running. "Ryan, what happened?"

"They've got Becka."

"What?"

"Becka—the Society—they took her."

Susan reached out and pushed aside his wet, black hair to examine the gash in his forehead. "Ryan, we have to get you to a—"

He shoved her arm away, then forced himself to speak calmly and evenly. "They've kidnapped Becka. They're going to hurt her. We've got to stop them."

Susan searched his face. He was dead earnest. "Where?" she asked. "How?"

"You said you knew some of the kids."

"One, yes. Laura Henderson. We were getting to be good friends. She even came over for dinner a couple of times. But now . . ." Her voice dropped off as she shook her head. "Things have been real tough for her."

"Do you know where they meet? Like, for their ceremonies and stuff?"

Susan frowned. "You think that's where they'd be? On a night like this?" There was a bright flash of lightning outside, followed by ominous thunder. Susan had her answer. Tonight was the perfect night. Without a word, she turned and started for the side office.

"Where are you going?"

"To call the police, to tell them where we'll be."

The goblet returned to the leader. It had made its rounds and now held the blood of all six satanists. Brooke lifted it high above her head.

"To you, great one, we offer our life's essence in exchange for your life's power."

There was another series of lightning flashes, some illuminating Brooke's face, some throwing her into eerie silhouette. The scene sent chills through Rebecca, yet she managed to hang on, refusing to give in to the fear. Then a Bible verse ran through her mind, and she began to recite it to herself over and over: *The one who is in you is greater than the one who is in the world. The one who is in you is greater than the one who is in the world. The one who . . .*

"And now," Brooke said, lowering the cup,

"for our final act of sacrifice." She nodded to the two hooded figures beside the table—Meaty Guy and Shaved Head. They reached for the pillowcase in the center. Meaty Guy opened it while Shaved Head pulled out its contents.

Muttly! Becka watched in horror as they tied ropes to each of his four paws. The little fellow whimpered pathetically until he spotted Rebecca. Suddenly his little ears perked up and his tail began to thump.

That was it. Becka could stand no more.

"No!" She screamed through the rag taped in her mouth. *"Noooo!"* She fought and kicked and squirmed for all she was worth. She fell into the mud, dragging down her two captors, Laura and Frail Girl, with her. They did their best to hold her, all the time shouting and swearing, but it did little good. Becka threw them off again and again until Meaty Guy and Shaved Head moved in to help.

In a matter of seconds, they had her in control. All but her mind. "Jesus!" she cried out. "Jesus, please! No! No! *Noooo!*"

Brooke began to laugh as the rain came down harder than ever.

They were in Susan's car. Ryan sat in the passenger seat fighting off the throbbing in his head, trying to take his mind off the pain in his chest. "Why'd you call the police?" he asked.

Susan frowned. "I'm sorry?"

"I thought everything was spiritual with you guys—just say your prayers and call fire down from the sky."

She gave him a look.

"Hey." He tried to smile. "I'm new to this."

Susan smiled back. "God uses the natural as well as the supernatural. Besides, not everything that goes bump in the night is Satan."

"That's exactly what I've been trying to tell Becka."

Susan nodded. "It's tricky to know the difference—I mean, to know what is truly supernatural and what is just man's doing."

"But you can tell?" Ryan asked.

Susan shook her head. "Not usually. But the tools, the weapons of warfare, are pretty much the same. It doesn't matter whether you're fighting against spirits or against flesh and blood."

Ryan looked at her, waiting for more. She continued.

"Our primary weapons are God's Word and our faith and love."

Ryan seemed surprised. "That's it? No supernatural hocus-pocus?"

Susan chuckled. "Once in a while, maybe. But it's not as often as you'd think. Oh, and we have one other weapon. In fact, it's our most powerful."

"What's that?"

"Prayer." She threw him a glance. "Mind if we do a little of that now?"

Ryan shook his head. "I wouldn't mind if we did *a lot* of that."

The storm reached the height of its fury. A giant blast of wind suddenly blew out all the candles, even the one stuck onto the skull. The rain came down at a sharp angle. Lightning continued nonstop, illuminating the scene like a thousand flashbulbs.

Becka was held fast by Meaty Guy and Shaved Head. Laura and Frail Girl had moved to the boys' places at opposite ends of the altar. Laura finished tying the last rope to Muttly's paw, then she and Frail Girl pulled the ropes taut, stretching the puppy spread-eagle across the table as he whimpered and whined.

Becka fought and thrashed, but it did little good. Meaty Guy and Shaved Head held her tight. She caught a glimpse of Brooke approaching Muttly, her arms raised high into the air, the wind whipping her sleeves.

Lightning flashed, revealing the dagger in her hand.

God! Becka's mind screamed. *Jesus, please!*

And then, just before the knife started its plunge, there was light—bright, moving light, coming through the bushes from the parking lot.

"It's a car!" Shaved Head shouted. "Somebody's here!"

Laura and Frail Girl started, momentarily loosening Muttly's ropes. In a flash, he scampered to his feet.

"No!" Brooke shouted. "We must complete the sacrifice!"

Car doors slammed and faint voices could be heard under the thunder: "Becka! Rebecca, can you hear me?"

"Let's get out of here!" Shaved Head shouted in a panic. The others agreed. All but Brooke.

"Becka! Rebecca, are you in there?"

The group continued to panic. Brooke shouted over them, "Pull those ropes tight! We must complete the sacrifice! We must complete the sacrifice!"

As Rebecca watched their panic grow and spread, the most unusual thing happened: She slowly began to feel a type of peace, a confidence. Granted, the two boys still held her fast, and Brooke was still preparing to kill her dog. But somehow, someway, a gentle peace settled over her . . . a calm confidence.

Jesus, show me what to do. Show me. . . .

As she prayed, the confidence spread through her body, allowing her to relax. The two boys felt her struggling ease and unconsciously loosened their grip. Not much, but enough.

With the fear gone, Rebecca was able to focus her thoughts. They became crystal clear. She knew what to do.

Muttly was starting to get away. Brooke caught one of his ropes with her left hand and jerked the animal toward her. She raised the dagger over him with her other hand. She was about to carry out the sacrifice on her own when Rebecca made her move.

It was instant. Catching the guys off guard, she leaped to her feet and threw herself at Brooke with all her might. She was still encased in the white nightgown and her leg was still in the cast, but she lunged across the circle and hit Brooke like a flying torpedo. The two bounced against the table, and the dagger flew out of Brooke's hands as they fell hard into the mud.

"Get her off!" Brooke cried. "Get her off!"

A flash of lightning illuminated the area,

and they both saw the glint of the blade just a yard away. Brooke reached for it, but Rebecca was already spinning her body around. Before Brooke could grab the weapon, Rebecca smashed her cast down with all of her weight, directly onto Brooke's hand.

"Augh!" Brooke screamed and grabbed her hand.

Rebecca moved her leg to the dagger and slammed down on it again and again, driving it deep into the mud.

Lightning flashed as Ryan and Susan raced around the bushes and entered the clearing. "Becka! Rebecca!"

Out of breath, Becka started to answer, but suddenly she felt a powerful arm grab her and wrap itself around her neck. It was Laura. Becka felt the sharp, cold steel of a dagger against her throat.

"Go away!" Laura screamed at Ryan and Susan. "Leave us alone!"

Brooke sat in the mud to the right of the altar, holding her crippled hand. Becka and Laura were sprawled in front of the altar, locked in a deadly embrace.

Susan recognized Laura instantly. "Laura . . . Laura, is that you?"

"Leave us alone!" she shouted again.

"Laura, what's going on? What are you

doing?" Susan took a step toward the girl, and Laura pulled Becka closer, pushing the knife more firmly against her throat.

Susan froze.

"No one asked you to come!" Laura screamed. "Get out of here!"

Lightning lit the clearing.

"Laura . . ."

"Kill her!"

All eyes shot to Brooke. She was on her knees, holding her hand, seething in rage. "Kill her! Make the *ultimate* sacrifice."

Laura's eyes locked on Brooke. She seemed unable to look away.

"Kill her! Kill her!"

Susan edged closer. "Laura . . . don't listen to her."

"I command you to kill her!" Brooke shouted.

Laura stared at Brooke, mesmerized, held by her rage, her power.

"Laura," Susan continued softly. "Listen to me, Laura. Don't let her tell you what to do."

The words tugged at the girl, nearly drawing her eyes back to Susan, but not quite. She couldn't look away from Brooke.

A police siren began to scream in the distance.

"Laura, I'm on your side."

Laura's eyes faltered, then shifted to Susan.

"Kill her!"

Her eyes darted back to Brooke, whose face was contorted with hatred.

"I command you to make the ultimate sacrifice!"

"Laura, I'm on your side. Laura."

No response. The siren grew louder.

"Laura . . . Laura, I love you."

Laura's gaze returned to Susan. The girl was scared, confused—pleading for help.

"I own you! Obey me!" Brooke's voice raised to a screech.

"Laura—" Susan took a step closer—"there's more to life than this."

"Obey me or I'll destroy you!"

Laura's eyes shot back to Brooke. She would not, she could not disappoint the leader.

"Laura, look at me . . . look at me. . . . I'm here to help you—I love you." Susan edged closer. "There's no power here. She has no control over you."

"I'll destroy you!"

"I love you." Susan's voice remained calm and in control. "Laura, God loves you."

Laura looked back to Susan. She was trembling, trying to hold back tears.

Susan continued, "I'm your friend, Laura, you know that. I love you."

"Obey me!"

"I love you." Susan started to move in again, her voice soothing. "Laura, I love you."

Suddenly Laura pulled Rebecca closer.

Susan slowed but did not stop. "I'll do whatever I can to help you, you know that."

Laura's eyes were blinking rapidly; the tears were coming faster. She turned to Brooke.

"Obey me! I'll destroy you! *I'll destroy you!"*

Then to Susan.

"I love you!"

"I'll destroy you!" Brooke's voice rose in fury, but Laura did not look back. Her eyes remained fixed on Susan.

"I love you, Laura. I want to help you." They were less than three feet apart. "Give me the knife, Laura. Give me the knife so I can help."

"I curse you!" Brooke screamed. "I cast your life into everlasting darkness! I curse you!"

Susan reached out her hand. "Just give me the knife so I can help. I love you."

Ever so slowly, Laura reached out her trembling hand.

Panic filled Brooke's eyes. She began to scream, "Hate your enemies with your whole heart, and if a man smite you on the cheek, smash him on the other!"

Laura hesitated.

Brooke rose to her feet, motioning for her followers to join her. "Hate your enemies with your whole heart . . ."

But they would not participate. Meaty Guy, Shaved Head, Frail Girl . . . they all looked away.

The siren grew louder. The police were practically there.

". . . and if a man smite you on the cheek, *smash* him on the other!"

"Give me the knife, Laura," Susan repeated. "I love you. Jesus loves you."

"Hate your enemies with your whole heart, and if a man smite you on the cheek, smash him on the other!" Brooke stood there, holding her hand, trembling in rage.

Laura was sobbing. Ever so slowly, she released the dagger. It fell into Susan's palm. Instantly, Susan dropped to the mud and threw her arms around Laura.

Rebecca scooted out of the way as the two hugged. Ryan was at her side in a second, his arms around her, holding her so tightly she could scarcely breathe.

Laura leaned into Susan and cried like a lost, frightened child. "It's OK," Susan whispered. "I love you, I love you. Sshh, now." She was crying, too.

All watched in silence as Susan and Laura remained on their knees, sobbing and holding one another, their tears mixing with the rain and the mud as the police car pulled into the parking lot, casting blue and red lights on everyone's faces.

11

"I should have been there," Scott said, shaking his head. It was almost 4:00 A.M. He sat in the emergency-room lobby with Becka, Susan, and Muttly, whom he'd smuggled into the building inside his zipped-up coat. "If I'd been there, none of this would have happened."

"I wouldn't be so sure of that, little brother," Becka said. She was back in her wheelchair. Her leg and collarbone had already been checked. The wet, soggy cast had been removed, and a new one had been applied. Now they were all waiting for Ryan. Becka continued, "Those guys had been planning it for days. You wouldn't have been able to stop them."

"Still, if I had been over at Darryl's like I said—" Scott looked to the ground, unable to finish the sentence.

Mom had returned from calling Ryan's parents. She reached out and rested her hand on his shoulder. They had already been through his deception, and the punishment had already been given out—something about being grounded until the year 2070. Now it was time to let him know he was still loved. Very much.

"I don't know what came over me." He kept staring at the floor.

"Good old-fashioned lust," Susan volunteered. "It's something even the best of us have to fight."

Mom nodded. "The important thing is that you won."

"Barely." Scott looked up and sighed.

"'Barely' counts," Mom said.

"I wanted to stay so bad. But as soon as

she told me her folks were gone, something inside clicked. I was out of there in about three point two seconds."

"And that's good," Susan encouraged.

"Yeah, till it gets around to everyone. Then I'll be the All-School Joke."

"But not with God," Mom said.

"Or with me, Scotty."

Scott glanced over at Becka. Her smile was full of pride. It helped, but not enough. "Besides," he complained, "I missed seeing you guys pull out the big guns against the Society."

Susan shook her head. "Like I told Ryan, whether we're fighting real spirits or just our own flesh, the weapons God gives us are still pretty much the same: prayer, Scripture, righteousness, faith—"

"And love," Becka concluded.

Susan looked at her and nodded. The group fell silent as all thoughts returned to Susan and Laura hugging each other down in the mud.

Becka looked at Susan and asked what was on everybody's mind: "You think Laura will be all right?"

Susan answered, "I hope so. The police have called her mom. I'm going down there just as soon as we get word on Ryan."

Becka sighed, "It was all just a mind game,

wasn't it? Just a way to scare me. They really didn't have any power."

"They thought they did," Mom answered. "But in all truth, probably not."

"Just the power of your fear," Susan added.

"And as soon as I was able to control that. As soon as I put my faith back in God—"

"You won," Scott finished the phrase.

"Seems to me you had a little help from your friends," a voice commented.

All eyes turned to the hall as Ryan appeared around the corner. He sat in a wheelchair with a large bandage over his forehead and his right arm in a cast.

"Ryan!" Becka cried in alarm as she started toward him.

He broke into one of his famous heart-breaker grins.

"Oh, Ryan," she said, blinking away tears. "What happened?"

"Just a mild concussion." He smiled.

The nurse who was pushing his chair toward the group continued as if reading a shopping list: "And two cracked ribs, a chipped elbow, a broken arm, a lacerated forehead, and a bruised shoulder."

"Just trying to keep up with the Williamses," he laughed as he pulled up beside Becka.

"His and hers wheelchairs," Scott observed. "Pretty cool."

"Now we can do races," Ryan teased.

The nurse cleared her throat. "Actually, we'll want to keep him overnight, for observation."

"Oh, Ryan," Becka said sympathetically.

"It's no big deal."

"But you did all this for me. You're like a hero."

The group oohed and ahhed.

"I think I'm going to get sick," Scott groaned. Suddenly Muttly began squirming and whimpering inside his jacket. The nurse stared at his stomach in shock.

"It's just a little indigestion." Scott smiled sheepishly.

Ryan continued talking to Becka. "I'm sorry you had to go through all that. I wish I could have stopped them at the house."

"You were terrific," Becka insisted. "When I heard your voice out there in the park, I knew I wasn't alone. Something came over me—like a strength or power or something. Without you it never would have happened."

Ryan shook his head. "It wasn't me."

She looked at him as everyone became silent.

"What I saw there tonight—the faith, the power—" he glanced over to Susan—"and the love . . ." He shook his head again. "I've never seen anything like it." Then, reaching beside his leg, he produced the Bible Mom had given him earlier that evening. "I haven't read this yet, but if what I saw tonight is anything like what we talked about over dinner, I think I'm about ready to sign up."

"Ryan." Becka's heart leaped. The news was too good to be true. She wheeled her chair closer. "Are you sure?"

"I've still got some reading to do—and by the looks of things, I'll be having plenty of time for that—but so far, so good."

Muttly could no longer be contained. He squirmed from Scott's coat and leaped to the floor. Scott tried to catch him, but the little guy scampered straight for Becka.

She reached down and scooped him into her lap. He began covering every inch of her face with wet, sloppy kisses. Ryan and the group laughed. Hearing Ryan's voice, Muttly spun around, saw another target, and leaped over the wheelchairs to start a second attack.

More laughter as Ryan coughed and sputtered. Yet he was not too busy to reach out and take Becka's hand. She felt him give her a little squeeze. She returned it, her heart bursting with joy.

Back at the Williamses' house, a message was forming on Scott's computer. A message that came quickly and urgently:

New Kid . . . Rebecca . . . Are you there?

There was a pause as the sender waited for an answer. Finally another message appeared:

There is a deserted mansion across town.
Rumor is that it's haunted. My sources say
the Society may challenge you to visit it.
Exercise caution. I repeat, be very, *very* careful.
The battle may be over, but the war rages on.

Z

Information on teen sex, AIDS, and condoms came from the following sources:

Pg. 88: Duane Crumb, "A Guide to Positive HIV/AIDS Education" (American Institute for Teen AIDS Prevention), 36–37. See also *Sex, Lies & . . . the Truth* (Wheaton, Ill: Tyndale House Publishers/ Focus on the Family, 1994).

Pg. 88: Bill Myers, *Hot Topics, Tough Questions* (Wheaton, Ill.: Victor Books, 1987) 91–93.

Something is waiting to be set free.
Some say it's the ghost of a little girl,
trapped in limbo. Becka and
Scott know that's not true.
What they don't know is it's
waiting for them, too . . . and
it's out to destroy them.

AUTHOR'S NOTE

As I continue writing this series, I have two equal and opposing concerns. First, I don't want the reader to be too frightened of the devil. Compared to Jesus Christ, Satan is a wimp. The two aren't even in the same league. Although the supernatural evil in these books is based on a certain amount of fact, it's important to understand the awesome protection Jesus Christ offers to all those who have committed their lives to him.

This brings me to my second and somewhat opposing concern: Although the powers of darkness are nothing compared to the power of Jesus Christ and the authority he has given his followers, spiritual warfare is not something we casually stroll into. The situations in these novels are extreme to create suspense and drama. But if you should find yourself involved in something even vaguely similar, don't confront it alone. Find an older, more mature Christian (such as a parent, pastor, or youth leader) to talk to. Let them check the situation out to see what is happening, and ask them to help you deal with it.

Yes, we have the victory through Christ, but we should never send in inexperienced soldiers to fight the battle.

Oh, and one final note. When this series was conceived, there were really no bad guys on the Internet. Unfortunately that has changed. Today there are plenty of people out there trying to draw young folks into dangerous situations through it. Although the characters in this series trust Z, if you should run into a similar situation, be smart. Anyone can *sound* kind and understanding, but their intentions may be entirely different. All that to say, don't take candy from strangers you see . . . or trust those you don't.

Bill